'Bye, Paget,' O'Malley called.

'Paget?' he exclaimed in astonishment, swinging back to face her.

'Isn't that your name?' she asked, surprised. That had simply never occurred to her, and she gave a little gurgle of laughter.

'No,' he said drily. 'Why should you think it was?'

'Because I heard the girl in reception call you that.'

'Oh.' Then, with a little grin that was quite utterly delightful, he declared, 'But it will do.'

'It will do?' she repeated, laughing. 'You can't call yourself something just because it will do!'

'Can't I?' he asked wryly. 'I . . .' He froze in mid-sentence as the floor beneath their feet shivered. It was only a slight movement felt through the soles of the feet, and yet . . . Staring wide-eyed at her companion, a flicker of alarm ran along O'Malley's nerves, then she gave an involuntary cry as the shiver became a subterranean grumble.

'Oh, hell!' she whispered.

'Run!' he snapped succinctly, but, without waiting to see if she would obey, he caught her arm in a punishing grip and hurled her in the direction of the archway behind him.

UNWILLING HEART

BY

EMMA RICHMOND

MILLS & BOON LIMITED
ETON HOUSE   18-24 PARADISE ROAD
RICHMOND   SURREY   TW9 1SR

*First published in Great Britain 1989
by Mills & Boon Limited*

© Emma Richmond 1989

*Australian copyright 1989
Philippine copyright 1989
This edition 1989*

ISBN 0 263 76288 2

*Set in Times 11 on 12 pt.
01-8904-44942*

Typeset in Great Britain by JCL Graphics, Bristol

Made and Printed in Great Britain

CHAPTER ONE

SHIFTING her position on the boulder that seemed to be getting harder by the minute, she glanced at her watch. Where the devil was her father? Honestly, he was the absolute limit. 'I'll meet you there at five,' he'd said. Hah! It was now gone six. He'd persuaded her, against her better judgement, to come on this trip, and now he couldn't even be bothered to be on time. 'You'll be a great asset,' he'd murmured with a twinkle in those impossibly blue eyes that fifty-seven years of hard living had not dimmed. In a moment of weakness O'Malley had agreed, but then, it was very difficult to deny her father anything. When charm had been handed out her father had been first in the queue, and he'd used it shamelessly ever since to get his own way. A conservationist of the first order, he charmed or browbeat people into his own way of thinking. Which was why they were in Turkey now. A stretch of the coastline was being bought up by a property developer, whose name escaped her, she thought wryly, because she hadn't been paying sufficient attention, and who was intending to turn it into a holiday resort. The fact that her father was not Turkish, nor had any ties with Turkey, didn't in the least deter him from trying to prevent them.

Neither did it seem to cross his mind that the local populace might actually welcome tourists. If he decided that they shouldn't have a leisure complex, then a leisure complex they would not have, not if he could help it, anyway.

'No one must know why we're here,' he'd impressed upon her. 'You never know, the very person you're so innocently chatting to could be the person who has a vested interest in the project going ahead.' Which made everything exceptionally difficult. O'Malley was a very outgoing person by nature, warm, lovely and capable, and all this looking over her shoulder was having the severest effect on her nerves. Tossing back the thick mane of corn-coloured hair, that had been expertly layered to curl and wave to just below her shoulders, she glanced at her watch again and gave a rueful smile. She was going to have a long, tiring walk back into Sophia. Her own fault, she admitted—she should have had more sense than to dismiss the taxi. Her father was probably up the coast somewhere, quite oblivious of the time. It was also going to be a very wet walk, she decided, surveying the darkening sky, and she was hardly dressed for storm conditions. Her T-shirt and cotton skirt would be soaked in seconds.

Pursing her mouth, she turned her head to stare at the ruined monastery that seemed to be perched rather precariously on the edge of the cliff. It would afford some shelter, she supposed, and, as thunder rumbled menacingly in the distance and a few large spots of rain patterned the ground at her feet, she made up her mind. Hitching her bag more comfortably on to her shoulder, she got to her feet and hurried towards the old and crumbling archway. Moving cautiously inside, not altogether sure she wouldn't rather get wet, she stared into the great hall, a rather bleak and echoing reminder of the ancient past. Part of the high vaulted roof had fallen in and she could clearly see the angry, racing clouds which gave the rather unpleasant sensation of being on a tilting deck. Rubbing her arms to rid them of goose-pimples, she picked her way carefully through the rubble, only to halt uncertainly as she saw she wasn't the only occupant. A tall, dark-haired man was standing in the far archway, his back to her as he stared out into the now sheeting rain, and the set of his broad shoulders and the way he held his head seemed somehow familiar. He looked like the man she had seen briefly in the hotel earlier. The man with the derisory smile—although she *had* been exposing rather a lot of long, sun-tanned legs as she had emerged from the low-slung taxi, she remembered with a small smile. She'd only seen him for a few moments, and then not very clearly, yet it would be hard to forget that tall, rangy body dressed in dusty denim shirt and jeans, or that shock of dark hair that looked as though it hadn't seen a barber in months.

Paget, she remembered. The girl in reception had definitely called him Paget. Paget something? Something Paget?

At her noisy entrance, he swung round and she
stared, fascinated, at the carved, unshaven face. A
face that would instil fear rather than comfort. It
was almost gaunt, the cheeks hollowed, and the
look of irritation he gave her only endorsed her
thoughts. This man lived rough, dangerously, he
would know the game of life—probably even made
up his own rules—as she did, and her generous
mouth curved into a wry little grin. They could be
stuck here for hours until the storm passed, and
O'Malley certainly wasn't averse to passing the
time with someone as fascinating as this man.
'Hello,' she murmured, moving towards him.
'Haven't seen a tall, fair-haired man wandering
around, have you?'

'No,' he replied. 'Should I have done?'

'No—not really, it's just that I seem to have lost
him.'

'Careless of you,' he drawled, and O'Malley
grinned. Leaning her shoulder against the ancient
wall, she stared unashamedly at him. Even though
he was now relaxed and had moved to face her, she
was aware of the strength emanating from that
supposedly indolent frame.

'You're going to have a long walk back to
Sophia if you don't find him,' he remarked.

So, he'd seen her arrive, had he? Her eyes
twinkling with humour, knowing instinctively that
there was no danger of this man taking her
seriously, she agreed artlessly, then, with her eyes
at their most innocent, queried lightly, 'Unless
you're going my way?'

'Sadly, no,' he demurred.

'Ah, well . . .' she sighed. 'It was worth a try.' He had the sexiest voice, she decided, low, seductive. Unconsciously so? Deliberate? There was also a faint tace of foreign accent. Turkish? French?

Taking her by surprise, he flicked a finger carelessly against her cheek. 'Have a nice walk back,' he murmured drily. 'If you get bored waiting for the rain to stop, there are some quite interesting carvings on the far wall.' And with a languid lift of his hand he began walking away.

'Story of my life,' she teased to mask her disappointment. She thought she could have quite got to like Paget something or something Paget. 'Ships that pass,' she called after him. 'Bye, Paget.'

'Paget?' he exclaimed in astonishment, swinging back to face her.

'Isn't that your name?' she asked, surprised. That had simply never occurred to her, and she gave a little gurgle of laughter.

'No,' he said drily. 'Why should you think it was?'

'Because I heard the girl in reception call you that.'

'Oh.' Then, with a little grin that was quite utterly delightful, he declared, 'But it will do.'

'It will do?' she repeated, laughing. 'You can't call yourself something just because it will do!'

'Can't I?' he asked wryly. 'I . . .' He froze in mid-sentence as the floor beneath their feet shivered. It was only a slight movement felt through the soles of the feet, and yet . . . Staring wide-eyed at her companion, a flicker of alarm ran along O'Malley's nerves, then she gave an involuntary cry as the shiver became a subterranean grumble.

'Oh, hell!' she whispered.

'Run!' he snapped succinctly, but, without waiting to see if she would obey, he caught her arm in a punishing grip and hurled her in the direction of the archway behind them.

They almost made it—were within sight of the open space beyond the arch when the ground suddenly heaved upwards, throwing them both off balance. If Paget hadn't grabbed her and shoved her sideways into the comparative shelter of the outer wall, she would have been killed. His hard, fit body rolled to cover her, his arms forming a protective barrier, and O'Malley forgot to breathe altogether as the remains of the roof tumbled to crash into the heaving floor.

The noise was indescribable, roaring, spitting, wrenching, rocks and masonry rumbling down around them, and with her face pressed painfully into her companion's chest O'Malley could only pray. And then it stopped. Just like that. With every sense stretched she stayed perfectly still, listening, her ears trying to pick up something, anything, then whimpered in fear as a piece of debris tumbled lazily from above, rolled a few yards and finally settled. His heart beating against her cheek seemed overloud, the arms holding her overtight, but gradually, when nothing else happened, they slowly relaxed their grip and O'Malley unfroze her muscles and allowed herself to breathe.

'Is it over?' she whispered, unglueing her eyes and staring into blackness. Complete, encompassing darkness. 'Was it an earthquake?' she asked tremulously.

'Does it matter?' he rasped back, his voice thick with the dust that covered them. 'Whatever it was, it seems to have effectively buried us. Are you hurt?'

'No,' she replied without even considering the matter. 'You?'

'No,' he said after a fractional pause. Then, with a long sigh, he levered himself cautiously away from her. 'And if your friend doesn't turn up, we shall have to rely on ourselves.'

'Yes,' she whispered. 'I hope I'm not claustrophobic.'

'You dare,' he warned softly. 'You just dare.'

'No,' she murmured ineptly. But how did she know she wasn't? She'd never before been in a situation where she might have found out. She got a bit panicky on the tube sometimes. Was that claustrophobia? 'Don't you think we can get out?' she asked in a small voice.

'Lady, I am many things,' he drawled with a tinge of exasperation. 'Unfortunately, being psychic is not one of them.' With a grunt, he got to his knees, then slowly stood, and O'Malley heard rubble crunch beneath his feet. Thank God she

wasn't on her own. She didn't think she would
have coped at all. He would. She got the feeling
this man would cope with anything, not like some
of the wets she was acquainted with. She couldn't
imagine Nigel of the city suits coping terribly well
in such a situation, and she grimaced as she
pictured the man who until quite recently had been
her constant escort, and wondered rather absently
why she always went out with men who were safe.
This man wasn't safe but, oddly, it wasn't a
thought that worried her.

Tensing her stiff muscles, she gradually stretched
her legs. When nothing disastrous happened, she
slowly sat up. She could extend her arms above her
head and sideways, she discovered. That was good,
wasn't it? Gaining confidence, she drew her feet
beneath her and slowly stood.

'We have about ten feet in which to manoeuvre,'
he said finally, as he carefully explored their
prison. She pulled a little face. She didn't think she
wanted to manoeuvre, didn't think she wanted to
do anything except keep still. However, if he
required them to manoeuvre, then manoeuvre they
probably would.

'I suppose we'd better do something about trying
to get out,' she murmured without much
conviction.

'What would you suggest?' he asked drily.
'Levitation?'

'Don't be silly,' she mumbled absently, suddenly
finding she had the most insane desire to giggle.
Shock, she supposed vaguely; then, finding her

brain devoid of any constructive thoughts, she leaned back against the rocks behind her. He seemed to know what he was doing, it was probably best to leave it all to him.

'Right,' he eventually continued in the sort of encouraging tone that one uses for five-year-olds when you want them to do something you know damned well they don't want to do, 'I would guess that the upright of the archway has fallen to create a roof above us, which means that hopefully we will be able to move the rocks to one side of it.'

'On the other hand,' she mumbled pathetically, 'we might not.'

'You want to hold a discussion on this?' he asked conversationally.

'No, of course I don't! I . . .'

'Then be quiet,' he said mildly.

'I was only going to suggest . . .' she began, only to be interrupted.

'You know how to get out?' he asked with soft sarcasm.

'No. Do you?' she asked sweetly. After a rather pregnant pause, he gave a grunt of laughter.

'No,' he admitted. 'But chauvinistic pride decrees that I have to know best, and I certainly have no intention of sitting here waiting to die.'

'No,' she said soberly. 'I'm sorry. I expect it's terror talking, or panic or something.'

'Maybe. However, I get the feeling it's only temporary. I don't imagine you stay down for long.'

'No,' she agreed, praying he was right, then gave

a small rueful smile. Certainly it had been true of her up till now; she never usually waited for anyone's direction. Headstrong, beautiful, full of fun and laughter, one of the golden people—or so her father always said, but then he was biased. She hoped he still was, then pushed thoughts of him very firmly away, knowing that to think of him now would be her undoing—and she didn't think her companion would be very tolerant of feminine hysterics. In fact, she didn't think the fact of her sex would sway him at all. Equality was probably about to come to cave-dwellers. Taking a deep, steadying breath, she said with only a hint of a tremor in her voice, 'I'm OK now. My stiff upper lip is back in place.'

'Good. Now . . .'

'You're not English, are you?'

'No,' he returned with some impatience. 'French. And,' he added, as though trying to forestall any other inane remarks she was about to utter, 'I promise you my upper lip is every bit as stiff as any Englishman's.'

'I didn't doubt it for a moment,' she mumbled on a thread of laughter, then sighed as he gently grasped her arms and turned her in the direction he wanted her to start.

'If we can squeeze through, all well and good. If we can't, we ease the rocks apart gently. I estimate the distance to be about fifty feet at most. All right?'

'Yes,' she murmured. 'Easy-peasy.' Although she guessed his estimate was meant to be comforting rather than accurate.

At first it wasn't too bad. The rocks seemed firmly wedged, with often enough space between for them to squeeze through; it was when the rain began seeping down to them that things became more difficult. The choking dust gradually turned to mud and the rocks which were mostly smooth granite became slippery so that they were unable to gain purchase.

'I knew it was a mistake to wear a skirt,' she muttered peevishly as the soft material caught yet again on an unseen snag, then swore fluently as she ripped her nail. Sucking her breath in sharply as pain stabbed along her hand, she put it in her mouth in an effort to ease the throbbing.

'What?' he grunted.

'Nothing,' she sighed. 'I broke my nail.'

His soft French expletive didn't really need any translation.

The further they moved, the more firmly the rocks seemed wedged, and they were forced to try varying directions. Bit by bit, O'Malley began to lose confidence. She didn't think they were going to get out, and her face grew bleak as she considered the very real possibility that this might very well become their grave. As her hand was grasped yet again and thrust into yet another crevice, she sighed drearily.

'Push,' he murmured.

'I am pushing.'

'Then push harder.'

Oh, God! Hours and movements blurred together as she pushed, pulled, shoved, despaired. Hours of choking, kneeling, crouching or sitting in an effort to find a place on her body that wasn't bruised or cut. Of prising at rocks with fingers that were raw and bleeding. Of muttering and swearing and cursing, of yearning for long, cold drinks, of wanting to strangle the man who forced her onward, ever onward. Of slipping and sliding backwards, of breath rasping in her lungs, of being wet and cold and hurting. For the past hour they had been silent, only grunts and curses to punctuate the stillness, or the occasional piece of debris that tumbled loosely, making them both freeze. As she had suspected, he made no concessions to her femininity.

'Stop,' he croaked, and O'Malley automatically stopped. 'Listen.' Straining her ears, she could just make out a shushing noise.

'What?' she mumbled indifferently.

'The sea.'

Turning her head towards him, she found she could see. Not much, but there seemed enough illumination to show her his eyes. For the first time since the earthquake, she could see, and she collapsed weakly, a shaky smile splitting her dirty face. 'Oh, Paget.'

'Yeah.'

As he manoeuvred the next large rock to one side, a glorious blast of fresh air bathed her face and she inhaled gratefully.

'Steady,' he warned, as she set to with a will to

finally free them. 'We have no way of knowing how far we are from the edge.'

'No,' she responded, and a horrid vision of them both plummeting into the sea forced her to slow down. That would be the final irony, getting themselves killed when they were within sight of freedom. When they finally crawled out on to sweet-smelling earth, O'Malley collapsed weakly, just breathing in the fresh clean air. Rolling on to her back, she stared up at the dark sky. The storm clouds had rolled away and the beautiful, beautiful heavens that she had thought never to see again were revealed in all their glory. Stars were beginning to wink out, and she lifted her wrist to look curiously at her watch, which incredibly was still working. Nearly nine o'clock. Almost three hours.

Turning her head towards her companion as she remembered that it had been his quick thinking that had saved her, she asked softly, 'Did I remember to thank you?'

'I took it as read,' he said with a rather dry inflexion, and she gave a grunt of laughter that almost turned to tears. Yes, that figured, she decided, he looked as though he might take most things in his life as read. A bit like her father—and she sent up a swift, silent prayer that he was all right. Although, knowing Nick, he probably would be—certainly, it was a thought she must hold on to. He'd be worried about her, though. At least, if he remembered where he was supposed to meet her he would be, she thought wryly, which wasn't at all certain. Was the village all right? She had no way of knowing that either, not at the moment. Sighing, she sat up. Paget was just a shadowy outline perched on the rubble, and she only gradually became aware that both his hands were clamped round his thigh.

'Paget?' she asked worriedly. 'Are you injured?' Crawling across to him, she peered at his leg, then gave a murmur of distress. 'How bad is it?'

'I have no idea,' he said tiredly. 'It feels like a damned great crater.'

'Nasty,' she murmured stupidly. About to ask him why he hadn't told her before, she changed her mind. There would have been no point, there was nothing either of them could have done while they were still buried. Without conscious thought, she tore off the ragged hem of her skirt and passed it across, then gave a weak smile as he grunted with laughter. Taking it from her, he tied it tightly round his thigh.

'Am I likely to be accused of being patronising if I tell you how well you did?'

'I did?' she asked surprised. Then, with a little spurt of humour, teased, 'Despite my rather inane remarks?'

'Despite the remarks,' he concurred.

'To be honest, I was beginning to think we wouldn't get out.'

'So was I,' he admitted.

'Oh,' she said lamely, then, with another shaky smile, murmured, 'I'm glad you didn't tell me.'

Giving another long sigh, he asked, 'Can you

drive?'

'Yes.'

'Yes,' he echoed, as though he had expected nothing else. 'Come on, then,' he added, getting awkwardly to his feet. 'If the damned truck's still there that is—and if there's a road left to drive it on.'

The truck was, the road wasn't. Where the road had been was a crevice, God only knew how deep. It was far too wide to leap across, even supposing either of them were in any fit state to leap, which they weren't. It also stretched into the distance as far as the eye could see. To Sophia? she wondered. Determinedly blanking out thoughts of the people of Sophia, she turned to look at the remains of the monastery which was now just so much rubble extending down into the sea. Turning dispiritedly away, she stared at the truck. She had noticed it earlier and had thought it a dumped wreck. 'That?' she asked incredulously.

'That,' he confirmed. 'It looks worse than it is.'

'Well, it could hardly be better, could it?'

Without bothering to answer, he limped wearily across to it, and O'Malley followed, finding to her horror that her body seemed reluctant to obey her commands. Her bones felt like rubber and she leaned gratefully against the rusty wing of the truck before making the mammoth effort to climb inside. Collapsing into the driver's seat, she sat and gazed almost blankly through the mucky windscreen. Even supposing it started, where were they to drive to? There was no road, not even a

track that looked negotiable, but his earlier praise
and his assumption that she was more than capable
of coping made it seem imperative that she at least
try. Had anyone else asked her to do it after having
just excavated herself from a ruin, she would have
laughed incredulously. As he put on the dim interior
light and handed her a bottle of warm brackish
water, she accepted it gratefully. It tasted like nectar
and she rinsed her mouth out two or three times
before swallowing some and handing the bottle back.

On the parcel shelf among the clutter was a
cigarette packet, the brand that Nick smoked, and
she squeezed her eyes tight shut to contain her sudden
tears. 'Please be safe,' she whispered. Taking a deep
breath, she picked it up and held it in her hand,
almost as though it might bring him closer. Finding it
empty, she flattened it out. At least it could be used
for something constructive. Reaching for the little
stub of pencil, she began to write a few words of
comfort—just in case Nick came looking, she didn't
want him to start shifting rubble in an effort to find
her broken body.

'Want a message left?' she murmured. When he
didn't immediately reply, she turned to survey him. It
was the first time she'd seen him clearly since the
earthquake, always before the light had been too
dim. His head was thrown back, his eyes closed, but
as she watched he rolled his head in her direction and
opened his eyes—and O'Malley got rather a shock.
They were the most beautiful eyes she had ever seen.
Green. Not the deep green of jade, but more like the
sparkling green of sea water, or an exquisite emerald,

and quite startling in that dirty face. For long, emotive moments she was unable to look away. His dark hair had fallen across his forehead to tangle with the dark brows that were drawn into a frown of pain, and she forgot for a moment what she had asked.

'No,' he said eventually, an eternity later. He seemed equally fascinated by her presumably dirty face, and for a long moment they just stared at each other. And then he smiled, a slow, tired, beautiful smile, and she smiled bemusedly back.

'Hello,' he said softly.

'Hello.'

Dragging her attention away from him with difficulty, and with a hand that shook uncontrollably, she picked up the tyre lever that was by her feet. 'Do we need this?' she asked huskily.

'No,' he said again, his eyes still fixed on her face.

Climbing out, she stumbled across to the pile of rubble. She felt totally uncoordinated, jerky, and it wasn't entirely due to her exhaustion. Something had happened to them both in those few minutes inside the cab, and she still felt the unfamiliar warmth and excitement. Propping the tyre lever in a prominent position, she attached her note to the top with hands that shook. Going back to the truck, she climbed inside.

'Where shall we go?' she asked softly.

'Thataway,' he said, equally softly, indicating with his head the direction he meant. She smiled faintly to herself; she didn't think he intended it entirely as a joke. 'Thataway' looked like an obstacle course for

drunks. But if that was what he wanted, who was she
to argue? Everything was beginning to take on a
dreamlike quality that she knew was exhaustion; her
body had been pushed far beyond its normal limits
and this was its way of slowing her down, coping.

'What did you put on the note?' he asked.

'O'Malley's OK,' she replied, turning her head to
give him a brief smile.

'O'Malley?' he queried.

'Mm. O'Malley.' She didn't think she had the
energy to explain that it was really Amalie.
Whichever way she said it, it always came out
sounding like O'Malley. So O'Malley was what she
was called. Groping round for the key and not
finding it, she sighed helplessly. It seemed to have
been a very long day.

'It's a knob. To the right of the wheel. Pull it.' She
pulled it and the engine coughed into noisy, shaking
life, shattering the peace. He leaned across and
snapped up a lever, and two pale beams groped out
into the night, which only further convinced her of
the folly of attempting to drive over that sort of
terrain.

'Are you really quite sure about this, my friend?'

'Yes. Just a bit longer, O'Malley,' he encouraged
softly, 'then we can rest.'

'Yes,' she muttered, because really there wasn't
very much choice. Behind was the sea and no road,
ahead were mountains that would probably defeat a
vehicle with four-wheel drive. Oh, well. It didn't
occur to her that they could have slept in the cab and
waited until daylight.

CHAPTER TWO

AFTER only a few miles of wrestling with the bucking, jumping wheel, her arms felt as though they were being wrenched from their sockets. If there was a hole, the truck made for it. If there was a rock, it hit it, and no matter how hard she tried to steer it between either she didn't succeed. Her teeth felt as though they were being shaken loose, and her eyes filled with helpless tears. She really didn't think she could go much further. Paget helped, adding his weight to hers on the wheel, and just when she'd decided she was going to give up she saw a light. Just for a moment, and then it winked out. Putting her foot on the brake, she came to a halt as she squinted through the windscreen.

'Don't stop.'

'But I thought I saw a light.'

'Then make for it.'

'Well, I would if it would go on again,' she snapped peevishly.

'It's ahead, slightly to your right,' he gritted, and she looked at him sharply. His jaw was clenched, his hand clamped round his thigh. Oh, hell!

'Don't bleed to death,' she muttered, and, taking a deep breath, she started off again, a small

23

suspicion growing in her mind. He'd directed her,
go right, left, whatever, which would
indicate—wouldn't it?—that he actually knew
where they were making for. Yet, when she'd asked
earlier, he'd merely said they were bound to find
something, as though it were a matter of luck not
knowledge.

However, she couldn't wrestle with two
problems at the same time; it was enough for the
present to keep them from rolling over on the
uneven ground. But she'd certainly have something
to say about it later. Steering as near as she could
remember towards where the light had been, bit by
bit she began to make out the outline of a house. It
was tucked away in the fold of the hill, and there
was even a track of sorts that seemed to approach it
from the other direction.

'Pull up in front,' he instructed, and she looked
at him suspiciously again. As soon as she'd set the
handbrake, he was out of the cab, and with a terse,
'Stay there,' he limped over to the doorway she
could faintly make out. Only, extraordinarily,
instead of knocking, he stood to one side, his back
flat against the wall. Frowning, she absently
switched off the engine and lights. What on earth
had she got herself into? As the door opened with a
caution that made her want to giggle, she strained
to hear what was said. Furtive. That was the word
for it. Fed up with being excluded, she climbed
wearily down. As she approached them, her face
clearly registered her bewilderment, both men
swung round. 'I told you to stay in the cab,' Paget

snapped. Then, with an impatient sigh, he pushed open the door and ushered them both inside.

As an oil lamp was lit she squinted against the sudden light. The room was clean, if sparsely furnished. A roughly made wooden table, four chairs. A sofa, an ancient armchair that had seen better days, and a blue fluffy rug that looked ridiculous. Heavy green curtains hung at the window. Beautiful home it was not.

Turning her head, she stared at the two men who were regarding her as though she were an unwanted piece of luggage that neither knew what to do with. Both were also very tense. If Paget looked like a pirate, then his companion looked even more unsavoury. He was short and stocky, with raggedly cut light brown hair and pale blue eyes.

'I don't suppose there's any tea in the offing?' she asked hopefully, and both men suddenly relaxed, almost as though she had passed some sort of test. Glancing speculatively from one to the other, she suddenly remembered Paget's injury and her eyes moved to his thigh. Her piece of skirt was still tied above the gaping wound that could clearly be seen through the torn jeans, although the material now was no longer blue, but scarlet with blood, and she sucked her breath in hard. 'We'll need hot water, bandages . . .' she began weakly. When neither man moved, only continued to regard her in silence, she stamped her foot in exasperation.

'You,' she said, prodding the shorter man on the chest, 'go and boil some water. 'You,' she said to

Paget, 'sit.' And, when he didn't immediately react, she dragged one of the wooden chairs away from the table and pushed him on to it.

Turning his attention away from her, he nodded to the other man, who then went with obvious reluctance into another room, which O'Malley could only assume was a kitchen.

'Going to tell me what's going on?' she asked as she struggled with the knot of material round his leg.

'No,' he said bluntly, one hand gripping the table hard as she quite obviously hurt him.

'Sorry,' she muttered. Gently parting the tear in his jeans, she stared at the deep gash. It loked horrendous, far too bad for her to cope with, and she raised troubled eyes to his. 'It needs stitching,' she said faintly.

'Can you stitch wounds?' he asked with dry mockery, his eyes reflecting the considerable pain he was in.

'No,' she shuddered.

'Then it doesn't need stitching,' he said flatly. 'Don't argue, O'Malley,' he grated harshly when she opened her mouth to do just that, 'just do the best you can.'

'I'm not a doctor,' she protested. 'I barely got my first aid badge in the Guides.'

'You can stop blood flowing, can't you? You don't need to be a brain surgeon to do that.'

Making a cross little grunt in the back of her throat, she got to her feet. 'You look terrible,' she retorted.

'Have you seen yourself?' he asked drily. Nodding to the far wall where a mirror hung, he watched as she walked across to peer at herself, then grinned at her exclamation of horror.

'Dear God, I look like a Gorgon.' She'd never have recognised herself. Her hair was matted and dark with mud, her face filthy, caked with dirt and blood. Her dark brown eyes, so unusual with fair hair, looked dull, lifeless. Putting up a hand to push her hair away from her face, she only then noticed how bad her hands were, and, as soon as she noticed that they began to hurt, and she cradled them against her chest. 'I'd better clean these up first before I touch your leg,' she declared. If it wasn't infected now, it soon would be if she touched it with hands in this state.

'Kitchen's through there,' Paget said, indicating with a nod of his head the room his companion had gone into.

Following his direction, she walked across. The other man had laid a tray with cups and saucers, and her lips twitched. The pair of them looked as though they knocked the necks off bottles; refinements such as cups and saucers seemed ludicrous.

'May I wash my hands?' she asked politely, and he turned to stare at her in astonishment.

'Only your hands?' he asked with a wry lift of one eyebrow, and she smiled.

'For the time being, anyway,' she replied, extending them for inspection, and felt vaguely comforted when he looked horrified. Abandoning his tea-making, he poured some water from the large saucepan on the stove into a bowl. Finding her soap and a towel, he offered, 'I'll light the stove and heat up enough water for a bath. What do you reckon about his leg?' he asked, indicating the other room much as Paget had done with a nod of his head.

'It needs stitching,' she said bluntly. 'However, seeing as the mention of such a possibility nearly brought on apoplexy,' she exaggerated, 'it looks as if either you or I will have to play doctor.'

'Then it will have to be you, miss,' he apologised hastily. 'The sight of blood makes me sick.'

'That figures,' she murmured wryly; she had often found in the past that the tougher-looking the man, the weaker he was when it came to illness. Paget just might prove the exception. Taking a deep breath and holding it in her lungs, she gritted her teeth and plunged her hands into the hot water. The pain was excruciating, and she leaned weakly against the stone sink until it had passed. When she opened her eyes it was to find him staring at her, his face as white as the towel he was holding.

'I'm OK,' she breathed. 'Tough as old boots is O'Malley.'

'O'Malley?'

'Mm. O'Malley,' she confirmed without explanation. If her mother weren't already dead, she thought she might have killed her for giving her such a stupid name,

'Stavros,' he offered, wrapping her hands gently in the towel.

'Hello, Stavros, I'm sorry for the intrusion,' she probed, but if she'd hoped for an explanation she saw she was going to be disappointed. As he turned away to pour out a cup of tea for her, she gave him a rueful little smile. Taking it, she drank it gratefully, then, emptying the bowl she had used, poured more hot water into it and carried it through into the other room while Stavros carried in the tea.

'Is there such a refinement as a medicine box?' she asked, staring rather worriedly at Paget. Beneath the dirt he looked grey. Glancing down at his leg, she saw blood was oozing thickly to soak his jeans.

'In the bathroom,' he mumbled without opening his eyes.

'I'll get it,' Stavros said hastily, and disappeared almost at a run.

Pouring out a cup of tea, putting in plenty of sugar, she held it out. 'Here, drink this, then do you think you could stand? We'll need to get those jeans off.'

Opening his eyes with obvious reluctance, he stared up at her, and a little gleam of humour lit the green depths. He had the longest lashes she'd ever seen on a man, thick and dark, fringing the beautiful eyes. He looked as though he could see into her soul. It was very disconcerting. To cover the confusion she suddenly felt, she retorted somewhat tartly, 'I have seen a man without his trousers before.'

'I didn't doubt it for a moment,' he murmured.

'However, I was merely wondering whether I was likely to fall over if I stood up.'

'Well, we won't know if you don't try, will we?' she asked sweetly, rather miffed. His words seemed to imply that she was used to seeing men in a state of undress. And she wasn't. Not used to it, exactly. Naturally, there had been one or two men in her life, she was twenty-eight after all, but not used to it. There certainly hadn't been a continual stream. 'Come on, Paget,' she said impatiently.

'Paget?' Stavros asked, astonished, and she whirled round to stare at him, but he was looking behind her, and whatever signal passed between the two men she didn't know. Suddenly Stavros gave a small grunt of laughter, and repeated drily, 'Paget.'

'I'm well aware that's not his name,' she said crossly, feeling excluded, 'but seeing as he won't tell me what it is, Paget will have to do. Now, will you please help him to stand up before he bleeds to death?'

Putting his empty cup down on the table, and placing his hands flat on the wooden surface, Paget levered himself upright. Stavros steadied him and O'Malley undid his jeans and eased them down, avoiding his eyes as she did so. She didn't quite think she would like the expression she was sure she would find there. As soon as they were below his knees, she indicated for Stavros to ease him down, then tugged them from his feet and tossed them aside. She hoped he had something else to wear, because those weren't going to be of any further use.

Pulling another chair up, she folded the towel on it before resting Paget's leg across it, and her eyes lingered for a moment on the hard-packed muscles. No soft living for this man, they were the legs of an athlete, powerful and strong. As he made an impatient sound in his throat, she hastily turned her attention to the wound. It looked awful. Dragging another chair round, she sat with the bowl of water on her knees and rather tentatively began to clean his thigh with the piece of clean rag that Stavros had found from somewhere.

'Don't stroke it, O'Malley!' he muttered irritably. 'If the pain becomes too bad, I'll yell. Believe me!'

Gritting her teeth, she did as he said, wincing every time he flinched. They had to change the water three times before O'Malley was satisfied that it was as clean as she could get it. Spreading antiseptic cream on a piece of lint, she held the edges of the wound together before placing it firmly on top, then bandaged it as tight as she dared. Paget was still conscious, but only just, she thought. Collecting more clean water and the flannel that was in the kitchen, she carefully sponged his face and hands. He was one of the most attractive men she thought she had ever seen, and if her hands lingered a little longer than was necessary over the task, then no one was unkind enough to mention it, although she blushed scarlet when Paget unexpectedly opened his eyes.

'Thank you, Nanny,' he said softly, and with a small smile he kissed her nose, the only part of her that he could reach without moving. Feeling the most peculiar dip in her stomach, she straightened.

'He needs to sleep,' she mumbled to no one in particular.

'Yes,' Stavros agreed, and something in his voice made O'Malley turn to look at him. He was staring down at Paget with a rather odd expression on his face, but when he saw her staring at him he turned away. That he cared a great deal for Paget was obvious, but there had been something else—compassion? A puzzled frown pulling at her brows, she carried the bowl into the kitchen where her own tiredness caught up with her. As she swayed, she was forced to hold on to the draining board until the nausea passed. There was a pump over the sink, and she pushed the handle down experimentally, to be rewarded by a jet of clear, cold water. From a well, she supposed vaguely. Sluicing her face, she dried it carefully before staring curiously at the other two doors in the kitchen. One obviously led outside, but the other? Cautiously turning the handle, she peeped inside. Bathroom. A large wooden tub sat against the kitchen wall, and she saw a pipe extended through it from the stove. Instant hot water. In the opposite corner was a wooden partition, and behind it a chemical toilet. Well, that solved one problem. At least she wouldn't have to venture outside to perform bodily functions.

When she walked back into the other room, there was no sign of Paget, and she looked queryingly at Stavros.

'Bed,' he explained, and she wondered at his obvious air of embarrassment until he added awkwardly, 'There's only one, and—er—Paget should—don't you think? You could use the couch, and I could push two chairs together.'

Eyeing the one sagging armchair and the wooden upright chairs and then Stavros's stocky body, she murmured, 'No. You take the couch.' Then, almost too tired to stand any longer, she asked, 'How big is the bed?' and before Stavros could stop her she walked across to the other door she hadn't investigated. Pushing the door wide, she stared in astonishment. Paget was lying on his back; either he'd undressed himself or Stavros had done it for him, because his naked chest rose above the quilt. But it wasn't the fact of his nakedness that astonished her, it was the fact that a small girl was cuddled in the curve of one arm. Paget's daughter? Turning her head, she stared at Stavros, only he wasn't about to explain—he made that very obvious. Another puzzle to add to her collection. Oh, well, life today had certainly been different. The bed was plenty wide enough to accommodate herself and, far too tired to care what Stavros thought, she murmured, 'I'll sleep here.'

Nodding reluctantly, he closed the door behind her. Removing the tatty remains of her skirt and pulling her T-shirt over her head, she climbed carefully into the bed and was almost instantly asleep as emotional and physical exhaustion caught up with her . . .

*   *   *

When she woke the following morning, two pairs of identical green eyes were staring at her, and she blinked in confusion. Not quite identical, she saw, one pair were a lot younger and set in a round, freckled face framed by long brown hair. 'Your daughter,' she whispered as memory rushed back. Attempting to move, she groaned and fell limply back, her eyes closing. She felt as though she had been beaten all over. When the pain had subsided to a near bearable ache, she opened her eyes again. They were still watching her.

'Why are you both staring at me?' she exclaimed, trying to encourage saliva into her parched mouth. God, she felt awful. They never did answer because at that moment the door opened to admit Stavros carrying a tray of tea. Dragging herself awkwardly up and stuffing the pillow behind her, she accepted the cup that Stavros held out with a grateful smile. He only seemed to smile back when he had got Paget's approval for the operation, and she turned to stare at him curiously, only to receive a look of such bland innocence that she pursed her lips in exasperation. In the light of day, he was even more attractive than she remembered, and she widened her eyes innocently when he gave a knowing smile. It was to be expected, she supposed; men who looked like that would be used to women giving them the eye. It didn't necessarily mean he was conceited, just that he was knowing. She was grateful when Stavros gave her thoughts a new direction.

'I've run a bath for you, miss,' he intoned formally. 'I expect you'll be stiff.' She nearly choked on her tea. He sounded like a well-bred butler, and anyone who looked less like a butler would be hard to imagine.

'Thank you,' she murmured, keeping her face straight with difficulty. God, her father would never believe this—and then, as she remembered that she didn't actually know if he was alive or dead, her eyes darkened with pain.

'I've also put out one of Mr—er—Paget's shirts for you to use until we can get you some clothes.'

'Thank you,' she said again, glancing at Paget to see how the appropriation of one of his shirts was being received, then looked hastily away again as she found he was gazing rather pointedly at her breasts, which were only flimsily covered by her lace bra. Flushing, she dragged the quilt up to cover them. Did he think his daughter was about to be corrupted by the sight of them? Or had he been more concerned about Stavros? Perhaps Stavros was a sex maniac on the run. Perhaps they were both sex maniacs on the run. Sighing crossly, she put her empty cup down on the side-table and, ignoring both men, climbed brazenly out. To hell with them, she was going to have a bath.

Rinsing out her underwear in the basin, using some of the bath water for the purpose, she hung them at the window. By the time she'd had her bath they should be dry. Scooping out a jugful of water to rinse her hair with and standing it in the basin, she climbed in, a little smile on her mouth.

Modern it was not. She'd never actually encountered a wooden bath before but, surprisingly, it was quite comfortable. Round and just wide enough for her to sit legs extended. She soaked for a long time before rousing herself sufficiently to wash, and she carefully examined her knees and hands. Neither had fared very well—or rather both *had* fared very well, she rectified to herself. It depended which way you looked at it. She could have been dead. Despite the house being spartanly furnished, it had been well prepared for occupation, even down to shampoo, and she gratefully washed her hair until all the grit and dust had gone. She could only assume Paget had been living here already, in which case, why hadn't he said so? Why all the performance about directing her here? And what had he been doing in the ruins, anyway? It seemed a funny sort of place to go on your own when you had a young child to consider. Perhaps he was a smuggler. Was that why he hadn't told her his name? Or was he a criminal? There seemed something vaguely familiar about him too, as though she might have seen a picture of him at some time. Was he famous? Was that it? He'd grown his hair long and started a beard because he wished to remain incognito?

'Are you intending to spend all day in there, O'Malley?' Paget asked drily, rapping rather peremptorily on the door.

'Five minutes,' she said hastily. Dunking her head in the bath water to get most of the suds out, she got out and released the water, then stared in consternation at the tide mark. How did one clean the bath? Quickly rinsing her hair in the basin, conscious that Paget's patience wasn't likely to be inexhaustible, she then rubbed it as dry as she could before borrowing whoever's comb was on the shelf to comb it into some semblance of order. Her underwear was still damp, but it would have to do. Dragging on Paget's white shirt and rolling the sleeves up, she hastily buttoned it through. It barely covered her pants, she discovered; she'd better remember not to bend over too often.

Paget was in the kitchen when she went out, wearing a short towelling robe, and he gave her such a long, comprehensive glance that she blushed, which seemed to surprise him because his eyes narrowed slightly. The tug of magnetism that she had felt the night before in the truck was still there, and she shivered. She had thought then that he had felt something similar, but now she wasn't so sure. It was difficult to read anything from that still face. 'Sorry if I've been a long time,' she apologised huskily. 'How's the leg?'

'Fine,' he said absently, his eyes not leaving her face. 'Quite a transformation,' he murmured, one hand going out to touch her hair, and then unexpectedly he sighed. With a wry twist to his mouth, he asked, 'How do you feel?'

'A bit stiff.' She smiled. 'Sore knees, but apart from that, lucky.'

'Yes, we were damned lucky.' But there was no fervency in his voice, just a simple statement of fact.

'Entirely due to your quick thinking,' she said warmly, which didn't seem to please him in the least.

Shrugging, he muttered, 'Breakfast's on the table,' then pushed almost rudely past her and went into the bathroom.

'I'm sorry about the mess in the bath,' she called after him. His answer was to close the door in her face.

What was all that about? she wondered. Was it because his leg hurt? Only she found she didn't quite believe that explanation. The little girl was sitting at the table, a glass held between her palms. She had a milk moustache and O'Malley smiled.

'Hello.' When the little girl didn't answer, O'Malley seated herself opposite and helped herself to bread, butter, jam and a cup of tea. She was extremely hungry, she found. 'Not going to talk to me, huh? Can't say I blame you. Probably thought it was some scraggy old witch in your bed.'

Shaking her head, she gave a shy little smile before lifting the glass higher to hide her face. Eating hungrily, she chatted unconcernedly, allowing the child to either answer or not as she chose, and as her eyes flicked to behind her O'Malley turned to see Paget leaning in the doorway. He didn't look any happier than he had when he'd passed her going into the bathroom, and she stared at him curiously. His hair was wet and he'd combed it into some semblance of order, yet she somehow longed to see it cut properly. He still hadn't shaved, so she assumed he was growing a beard. He looked dark and dangerous, and she couldn't for the life of her understand why he didn't make her nervous. His beautiful eyes seemed to hold a rather feverish glitter, and she got hurriedly to her feet. Walking across to him, she put a hand on his forehead. It was burning up and, even though he shrugged irritably away, he didn't comment.

'Bed,' she said succinctly in her best nanny voice.

'I . . .'

'Bed, Paget. You're burning up. Don't argue. Where's Stavros?'

'Gone to find out how far the earthquake extends,' he murmured, and as he swayed she put one arm round him and urged him in the direction of the bedroom. As he lay down with a sigh of relief, she checked the bandage before covering him up. There was no sign of blood coming through, so she left it alone. Walking out, intending to see if there were any aspirins in the medicine box, she halted as she registered the little girl's terrified expression. Forcing a smile, she went across to her. Squatting down beside her chair, she laid a gentle hand on her knee. 'I'm sorry, darling, were you worried? Daddy has a bit of a headache. Will you sit with him for a minute while I find some aspirin?'

Nodding, she scrambled down and ran into the bedroom. Finding a couple of soluble aspirins, O'Malley dissolved them in water and carried them back to the bedroom. Paget had pulled himself up against stacked pillows and his daughter was kneeling beside him, nodding solemnly at something Paget had obviously just said. Perching on the edge of the bed, she proffered the glass.

'Must I?' he asked, pulling a face.

'Yes,' she said firmly. 'Mustn't he?' she asked the little girl, and she nodded. Looking back at her father, she grinned. 'And it's no good trying to outstare me, I'm a very determined lady.'

'I had noticed,' he said drily, swallowing the aspirins in one gulp and grimacing. 'God, they taste awful.' Handing her back the glass, holding her eyes with his, he asked slowly, 'Who are you, O'Malley?'

'Who?' she asked, astonished. 'I'm not sure I know what that means.'

'Why are you in Turkey, then?'

'On holiday,' she lied glibly, remembering her father's injunction. It would be just her luck if Paget turned out to be the property developer they were trying to avoid. Was that why he was reluctant to tell her his name? He needed as much secrecy as her father? There was a lot of money in property development, a lot to lose.

'How long for?'

'Two weeks.'

'And then?'

'Back to work.' She hoped. The magazine she worked for was struggling for survival, and at the moment there was no guarantee that there would be a job for her when she went back. Oh, well, something would turn up. O'Malley was nothing if not an optimist. She had taken her holiday early, at their request, which was why she'd been free to help her father out.

'Doing?' he persevered.

She could hardly tell him that she worked as a freelance writer for *Better Earth*, a conservation magazine, because if he was the property developer, it would be like red rag to a bull, and more difficulties she clearly didn't need. Neither did she want to antagonise him, she wanted to get to know him better. 'Nanny,' she invented quickly with a little grin as she remembered his words of the night before. Well, she had been once, and two more horrific children would have been hard to find. Little monsters. She'd spent a year in Spain with them and their wealthy parents, and it was a wonder she hadn't gone grey. Staring blandly at him, she could see he didn't believe a word of it, and she grinned. 'You?'

'I'm writing a book about the hill people. Kurds, you know.'

'Oh, yes?' she queried. 'How interesting.' And she could see he knew she didn't believe a word of his bit of fiction either, and she chuckled. 'How far is the village from here?'

'About twenty miles.'

'That far?' she exclaimed, surprised.

'Mm. And no guarantee that you'll actually get there,' he murmured somewhat mockingly, as though anticipating that she might attempt to walk.

'Might get kidnapped by Kurds, might I?' she teased. Shaking her head ruefully, she got to her feet. 'Want anything? A cup of tea?'

'Tea would be fine.'

CHAPTER THREE

WHEN she'd taken him his tea, O'Malley turned her attention to herself. Hopefully Stavros wouldn't be long, and then she could go and look for Nick. Opening the medicine box, she took out the scissors and with a great deal of ouching and ahhing cut her ragged and broken nails. The tips of her fingers were still sore, and she rubbed some antiseptic cream into them, then did the same for her knees. How far had they driven last night? she wondered. A walkable distance? Chewing worriedly at the inside of her lip, she debated the possibility of walking back to see if her note had gone; at least then she might be able to stop worrying. Putting the cream and scissors back in the box, she walked into the bedroom. Paget was asleep and she stood for a moment looking down at him. Just who the hell are you, my friend? she asked silently. Turning her attention to the little girl, who looked as though she would keep vigil over her father until time ended, she smiled.

'He'll sleep for a while yet. Want to help me clear up?' She desperately needed something to occupy her, and that would at least help take her mind off her troubles. Her question obviously took a few moments of careful thought. Staring solemnly at her, the girl finally nodded. With a last look at her father, she scrambled off the bed to join her at the door.

'Going to tell me your name?' she asked as she began clearing the table. But, when she merely looked worried, O'Malley didn't press her but carried on with her task. Had it been impressed upon her that she mustn't talk to strangers? Well, that was only right and proper in this day and age when so many terrible things happened to kiddies. 'My name's O'Malley,' she continued in her friendly fashion, and gradually, bit by bit, as she chatted unconcernedly about this and that, the child relaxed. She helped her carry things out to the kitchen, and while they waited for the water to heat up on the Calor gas stove for washing up, O'Malley searched for something to use as a duster. If her skirt hadn't been so filthy, she could have used that.

'Now, where do you suppose he keeps the broom?' she asked of her silent companion. Something must have been used previously because the cottage was quite clean, the floor swept. As the girl almost ran outside, O'Malley slowly followed. In the recess beside the kitchen door was a cupboard, and as she stood impatiently before it, a smile on her face, O'Malley tugged it open.

'Oh, well done,' she said warmly, staring inside. Not only were there cleaning materials, but two spare Calor gas cylinders, a stacked pile of wood, even a garden fork, she saw in amazement. She couldn't imagine that would be much use, one would need a bulldozer at least to make any impression on that stony ground. There was also an old car battery and a hose coiled on the wall; a veritable treasure trove, in fact. Taking out the broom and the open-topped box that contained dusters and polish, she murmured, 'Well, my lady, it looks as though we're in business.'

'It's Jenny,' she said shyly.

Smiling down at her, O'Malley held out her hand to be shaken.

'Hello, Jenny.'

'Hello,' she whispered.

Handing her a duster and taking one for herself, O'Malley led the way back inside. When they'd dusted, Jenny solemnly following her lead, she bundled up the revolting blue rug and handed it to her. 'Think you can give it a good shake outside?' And when she nodded and went off with it, O'Malley swept the stone floor. Must be hellishly cold in the winter, and she wondered just how long Paget had been here. She knew foreign nationals were only allowed to stay ninety days, she remembered how that had been impressed upon her, so presumably he hadn't been there too long. Sweeping the pile of dust out and through the kitchen, she shaded her eyes against the warm sun to stare towards the Taurus mountains. They were only in the foothills here, but even so the ground was rocky and bare. It must be very desolate up on the peaks. So why was Paget staying here in the middle of nowhere, with a young daughter who couldn't have been more than five or six? And where was Jenny's mother? Hearing a sneeze, she turned, then burst out laughing. Jenny seemed to have enveloped herself in the rug completely, all she could see of her was a tousled head.

'You look like a blue caterpillar,' she told her as she helped her unravel herself. Handing her the broom to hold, she gave the rug a quick shake before taking it back inside.

When they'd washed up, she made them both a snack, after which Jenny curled up on the sofa and promptly fell asleep. There were no personal possessions scattered around, no toys, photographs, nothing to tell a stranger who lived there. One or two books were balanced on a side-table, novels—one by Dick Francis, she saw. Unfortunately she'd already read it and she pulled a face. She liked his books. A couple of blankets were folded on the back of the sofa and, seeing there was nothing she could do until Stavros got back with the truck, she decided she might as well do a bit of serious sunbathig. She still felt stiff and sore, maybe the sun would ease her poor old aching back. Laying the blanket on the ground beside the whitewashed wall where she'd be full in the sun, she removed Paget's shirt and folded it for a pillow. There was no one to see, and, even if there had been, her underwear covered her as well as a bikini would have done. She wished belatedly she hadn't left her bag in the ruins, though, her moisturiser had been in there. Too many days of this and her skin would be like old leather. Fortunately, Nick had her passport—or she hoped he did, hoped he was in a position to have it, then hastily banished thoughts of her father. Worrying about him would do no good at all. She had to be optimistic, otherwise she'd go mad.

Lying on her back, she wriggled into a comfortable position and closed her eyes. She was just drifting pleasurably when a shadow blocked out the sun. When it didn't move, she opened her eyes. Paget was standing above her, dressed only in a pair of tatty shorts.

'Hello,' she murmured lamely, a little curl of excitement unfurling inside her. She wondered briefly whether modesty should decree she put his shirt back on, then with a mental shrug decided she couldn't be bothered. He'd already seen her half naked and hadn't exactly been thrown into a welter of passion. Unfortunately—the thought popped into her head. 'How do you feel?' she asked hastily, deciding it was too damned dangerous to set her thoughts along those lines. They were virtually isolated here and she'd have no protection at all if he turned nasty. So why wasn't she worrying? she thought wryly.

'Fine,' he answered, his eyes not leaving hers. Edging her over a bit with his foot, he sat beside her legs and she stared at the bandage encircling his thigh.

'How's the leg?'

'Fine,' he repeated drily. 'How are the knees?'

'Fine,' she echoed, her mouth curving into a delightful grin. 'Want me to change the dressing?'

'In a bit. I'll have a bath first, I've just put the water on to heat.'

'Want anything? Lunch?'

'Not lunch, no,' he drawled; then, taking her completely by surprise, he rolled on to his side so that his face was above hers. 'You look very tempting, O'Malley,' he said softly, and she shivered, then drew her breath in sharply as he trailed one hand lazily along her thigh to her hip. She should stop him, tell him she wasn't a girl like that—only, with him, she found she wanted to be and the thought didn't even horrify her. She certainly didn't push his hand away. It had been a long time since she'd felt such an overwhelming attraction for a man, and she wanted him to kiss her, she found. Touch her. His face was quite expressionless and for a moment she thought that she had misunderstood, that he was only mocking her, but then he lowered his head and lightly touched his mouth to hers—and an electric current shot down to her toes. Drawing back in shock, she saw he was smiling faintly, his beautiful eyes full of humour.

'Secret weapon?' she asked shakily, her body still tingling from the brief contact.

'Excess of electricity,' he whispered. Moving his hand to her jaw, he exerted gentle pressure until her mouth was exactly where he wanted it, then kissed her with a thoroughness and expertise that melted her bones, made her yield with a little sigh of contentment. This was what she wanted, had wanted since the first time she had heard his voice. Her eyes closed, she slid her hands slowly up his hard chest, her fingers revelling in the sensuous feel of warm male flesh. Up across his shoulders and neck to tangle in the hair at his nape, her thumbs exerting gentle pressure in the hollow behind his earlobes . . . She felt him shudder slightly against her. His kisses weren't urgent, but soft, gentle, producing a delicious languor.

When he drew back she stared up at him, slightly bemused. Moving her hand round to his jaw, she rubbed gently against the soft stubble. 'It tickles,' she murmured as she drew his head back down to hers.

Reality receded and there was only this, a warm, hard body against hers, an expert mouth touching and touching again, a warm tongue that explored lazily. When he drew away once more, his eyes making a thorough appraisal of her face, eyes, nose, mouth, she did the same, one hand brushing back the lock of dark hair across his forehead. 'I get the feeling that the shaggy hair and unshaven look aren't your usual style, my friend,' she said huskily, and he gave a slow smile that fascinated her. His teeth looked very white in that dark, tanned face, even and strong, the mouth well shaped, the lower lip slightly full, and she ran her forefinger across it. In reply, he placed the ball of his thumb on her chin below her lower lip and teased gently until her mouth parted, and his eyes darkened fractionally before he lowered his head again to tease the lip between his teeth. Just when she thought she could stand no more, he moved to the cord in her neck.

Her hands shaped the smooth muscles and contours of his back, then halted as she encountered a hard ridge of scar tissue. 'Old injury?' she queried, her voice slightly thick with passion.

'Mm,' he moaned unhelpfully as he continued his own exploration in a downward direction, until his mouth was against the creamy swell of her breast above the lace barrier of her bra and she forgot all about asking him how it had been caused.

'Is this wise?' she asked raggedly, her breathing somewhat erratic as he eased the lace to one side to expose the nipple to his seeking mouth.

'Probably not,' he mumbled as his tongue flicked erotically at the peak which was doing the craziest things to her insides. 'Want me to stop?'

'Hell, Paget, what sort of a question is that?' she asked, shaken. 'You know the answer as well as I do.'

'Mm. So I do.' With a little sigh, he tidied the lace back into place, and when she looked at him in some confusion, because that hadn't been at all what she meant, he grinned wolfishly, which made him look more than ever like a pirate. 'Not the time, nor the place—unfortunately. I don't want Jenny finding us in a . . .'

'Compromising situation?' she asked wryly.

'Mm. And if I don't stop now, whilst I can, she will.' Only O'Malley didn't believe him. This man would stop at any damned time he pleased, she thought, giving him a look of irony. There was a wealth of experience in that hard face, in those impossibly beautiful eyes.

As he lay down, folding his hands behind his head

and closing his eyes, she gave him a look of exasperation, and sat up. Putting the shirt behind her to keep her back off the hot wall, she leaned back and hugged her knees.

'Don't,' he murmured, and bright green eyes gleamed at her between thick lashes.

'Don't what?' she asked, bewildered, and a little chagrined that he seemed able to turn his feelings off without effort.

'Put your legs up. It's playing havoc with my—er—good intentions.'

'Turn the other way, then,' she muttered, but whether he had intended it or not, she now felt embarrassed. With a cross sigh, she wrenched his shirt out from behind her and put it on. 'Better?' she asked waspishly, and he grunted with laughter. Staring down at him, she found she had to forcibly restrain her hand from touching him. She wanted to smoothe the tangled hair off his forehead, touch that strong throat. His chest was hard and tanned, not the type of tan acquired on some holiday beach, the skin was too weathered for that, burnt by some desert sun, maybe. His stomach was flat, hard, not an inch of spare flesh on his lean frame. This man lived hard and probably dangerously, and he fascinated her. The legs were long and powerful and even relaxed, his beautiful eyes hidden from her, he looked coiled, wary, yet in a way complete. Tough, his own man, allowing nothing and no one to get in his way. He might smile and tease, drawl that sexy drawl of his, but it didn't fool her into thinking he might be soft. And, if he hadn't stopped, she would

have allowed him to make love to her.
Extraordinary. She'd never been promiscuous in her
life. Never leapt into bed with a man on their first
meeting, nor even on the second, yet would have
allowed this man intimacies previously unthought
of. Would have matched the passion that she knew
was in him. Yet she knew absolutely nothing about
him, not even his name.

'What are you doing here?' she asked bluntly.

'Researching the hill tribesmen, I told you,' he
mumbled sleepily.'

'Liar,' she muttered. His answer had again been
too glib, too pat, then knew she was right when he
grinned. Knowing the futility of pursuing it, she
asked instead, 'Why bring Jenny to this God-
forsaken place?'

'Don't you like it?' he asked infuriatingly. 'I
think it's splendid.'

'God, you're irritating,' she retorted, yet there
was an appreciative smile in her eyes. 'How far is it
to the ruin, then? Walkable?'

'No, O'Malley, it isn't. Why? Worried about
your friend?'

'Yes, a bit,' she confessed. 'I'd just like to be sure
that he's all right.'

'Probably is,' he said indifferently, then, opening
one eye, asked, 'Is he your lover?'

'Now, why should you assume that?' she asked a
trifle crossly. And, even if he thought he was, after
almost making love to her himself, couldn't he have
sounded just the teeniest bit jealous?'

'I didn't assume. I merely wondered.'

'Why?'

'Because, O'Malley, ladies like you usually have a string of lovers. You attract men like bees to a honey-pot.'

'Rubbish! And what do you mean, *ladies like me*? I'm no different from anyone else. And I do not have a string of lovers,' she said, peeved.

'Don't you? Hard to believe of a blonde Amazon with legs that start at the neck,' he murmured drily. 'Think I didn't see that little display outside the hotel?'

'It wasn't done for your benefit!' she retorted. 'Nor for effect. When you have long legs it's a little difficult to get elegantly out of low-slung taxis! And I am not an Amazon! I'm five feet ten. And don't do that!' she muttered as he smoothed one large palm down her skin, making her shiver with renewed awareness.

'Only admiring them,' he murmured. 'And don't tell me you don't like or expect to be admired, O'Malley, because I won't believe you.'

'I don't give a damn what you believe.'

'Now *that* I do believe!' he stated humorously. 'Go your own way regardless, don't you?'

'No, I don't!' But did she? He made her sound a very selfish sort of person, and she didn't think she was, or not entirely. 'I enjoy a certain measure of independence,' she said loftily, then gave a little gurgle of laughter as he opened one eye to regard her with comical irony.

'Kind to animals and children, too, I bet,' he scoffed, and she flicked one finger against his cheek in remonstration, before asking curiously,

'Where's your wife?'

'Dead,' he said flatly.

'Oh, sorry.' Well, that successfully brought that topic of conversation to a close. She didn't think he would appreciate her pursuing it, his flat tone had made that very clear. She also felt guilty. She hadn't given a thought to his wife earlier; she would have allowed him to make love to her thinking he was a married man, and that thought made her feel worse. She would never have thought herself the sort of person to come between man and wife. She hadn't known the woman was dead, so in effect she was guilty of that.

Not liking herself very much at that moment, she gave a long sigh, then stared up at the arc of blue sky. A lone bird was wheeling about above the hills. Looking for prey? she wondered. A dry wind stirred the dusty earth, and she watched a piece of paper flutter half-heartedly along the ground like a fledgling learning to fly. Even out here they had litter, and the thought saddened her. There would be more than litter if the land were developed.

'What's the matter, O'Malley? Bored?'

'More like frustrated,' she snapped, glancing at him from the corner of her eyes.

'Sorry I can't oblige.'

'No, you aren't,' she derided. 'Don't tell fibs.' Then, staring round her at the totally inhospitable terrain, she burst out, 'What on earth do you do all day? This total inactivity would drive me insane!'

'You should learn to relax,' he responded

indifferently.

'I don't want to learn to relax! I want to do something!' Getting irritably to her feet, she walked off round the corner of the house. God, he was infuriating. Pity they weren't on the coast; she could have gone for a swim, exercised some of the restlessness out of her, perhaps. Leaning back against the wall, she hugged her arms round her. Out of the sun, it was chilly and she felt her arms goose-pimple and her nipples contract. They seemed to ache and she sighed again. She didn't ever remember wanting a man they way she seemed to want him. Even when they'd been trapped in the ruins, his voice and touch had excited her. She felt so totally unlike her normal self, had behaved quite shamelessly—was it any wonder that he'd got the wrong impression of her?

To him, she was just a diversion—easy game, the unpleasant thought intruded—someone to while away a lonely hour. Well, maybe not even lonely, which made it worse, for she doubted Paget was ever lonely. Alone, but not lonely. And surely she wasn't turning into one of those women who expected adulation as their due. His words seemed to imply that he thought she did. She knew she was attractive to men, but surely she wasn't conceited enough to think it her due? The trouble was, she was spoilt. Not in a material sense, but she'd seen the best of manhood in her father, and very few men measured up to that indefinable something. Not that she wanted or needed a father figure, far from it, but Nick had always treated her as an equal,

capable of doing anything he could do, or within
reason, anyway. Then she gave a gurgle of laughter.
Reason very rarely came into her father's thinking;
he was impulsive, generous to a fault, quick to
anger, quick to forgive. But reasonable he wasn't.
Most men she met either idolised her or deferred to
her, neither of which made very satisfactory
relationships, which was presumably why she'd
reached the ripe old age of twenty-eight without
becoming emotionally involved. She could become
emotionally involved with Paget, she thought, and
that wasn't very wise.

Going to perch on a nearby rock, she put her chin
on her fists and tried a bit of total honest
assessment. Struggle and adversity were supposed to
form character—did that mean she didn't have one,
as she neither struggled nor adversed? If there was
such a word, which she doubted. Life had always
been kind to her, she realised. Apart from the death
of her mother when she was five, tragedy had not
touched her. Nick had brought her up to be as
independent, and possibly arrogant, she admitted,
as himself, much to the dismay of numerous female
relatives. She'd sailed through school, taking and
passing her exams with ease. She had enjoyed the
years at university, had never had trouble finding
enjoyable and fulfilling jobs. But she'd never
actually stuck at one, had she? she thought,
frowning again. Did that make her shallow? She
didn't know. She hoped not. She had plenty of
friends, enjoyed life, but would, she thought rather
wistfully, like to be married, have a family. Only

where were all the men? By men, she meant men of character and integrity, men of strength—like Paget. She liked him, she admitted that, could get to like him a lot more. Wanted him. Why? Because he presented a challenge? Intrigued her? No, she decided, because he seemed to answer a need in herself, seemed to offer her something she'd never felt before. Did you, could you, suddenly meet a person and know that he was the one you'd been looking for? Instantly know, with a gut feeling, that he was the one? And what happened if those feelings weren't reciprocated? Ah, there was the rub. Paget liked her, she thought, she amused him for some reason, but did he feel anything more? Certainly it would be dangerous to hope so, dangerous to assume he felt the same rapport she did. That way she could get hurt. It looked as though she was maybe going to find out about adversity, after all.

'O'Malley?'

Turning her head, she reluctantly pushed herself to her feet and walked round to see what he wanted. He was endeavouring to unwrap the bandage from his thigh, which was quite obviously stuck, and she tutted in exasperation.

'Don't tug it! You'll make it bleed again. And fancy doing it out here! Do you want it infected, for goodness' sake? Oh, come into the kitchen,' she said impatiently. Ignoring his look of mockery for her bossy tone, she helped him to his feet and urged him inside. 'Is the water hot enough for your bath?' And when he nodded meekly, she asked, 'Do you have any salt?'

'Salt?' he asked in astonishment. 'What do you want salt for?'

'To put in the water. It will help stop any infection.'

'Oh.' Reaching up, he took a packet out of the cupboard and handed it to her. Pulling a face, she went into the bathroom and tipped a liberal amount into the water.

'It will sting,' she warned.

'Thank you,' he said drily. 'I suspect that's why you're doing it.'

'Nonsense! It's for your own good.'

'Mm. I wonder why it is that everything that's for one's own good always hurts?'

'I've no idea,' she said shortly. 'Stop shilly-shallying and get in the bath.'

'Yes, ma'am. Are you staying?'

'Only to remove the bandage. Any other functions, you can perform yourself. If it makes you nervous, I won't look,' she promised, her lips twitching.

'Oh, I wasn't worrying about me,' he said blandly, and O'Malley felt like pushing him backwards into the water. She did, however, avert her eyes while he removed his shorts and got in, not that it stopped her vivid imagination, because it didn't. When she turned round, she burst out laughing. The flannel had been very strategically placed and, although his eyes were full of mocking audacity; they also showed the pain he was in. Sobering, she knelt and gently squeezed the bandage to make sure it was soaked right through, keeping her eyes very firmly on her task, she gritted her teeth in sympathy as his breath hissed inward in pain.

'Sorry,' she muttered. Taking a deep breath, she slowly began to unwind the bandage, easing it gently apart where it seemed stuck. The closer she got to the wound, the more stuck it became, and instead of white, the bandage was soiled a dirty yellow colour. Exchanging a worried glance with him, she finished unravelling it and then put it on the floor beside her. Catching the edge of the lint with her fingers and immersing his leg, she gently pulled.

'Don't play with it, O'Malley,' he gritted through his teeth, his breath held, 'just yank if off!'

'I can't,' she whispered, feeling slightly sick. With a harsh expletive, he put his hand over hers and pulled hard, and she stared at him worriedly as he groaned with pain. Unfortunately the force of his action tore the wound open, and blood and pus began to ooze out.

'Now look what you've done,' she whispered, staring at it in horror.

'It was no good leaving it,' he said weakly, his teeth clamped together. 'If it's infected it has to be cleaned out. I don't want to lose my damned leg just because you're squeamish.'

'No,' she said faintly, her face taking on the colour of chalk. 'What we really need are antibiotics.'

'Well, we don't have any,' he said harshly, and, taking the soiled lint from her hand, folded it carefully before using the clean edges to wipe off the muck oozing from the gash. Immersing his leg again, he leaned back with a sigh of relief. 'Let it soak for a while, then you can clean it up and re-dress it.'

'All right,' she agreed weakly. 'I'll go and look out some more bandages.'

Going back into the main room, checking that Jenny was still asleep, she slumped at the table. She still felt slightly nauseous and to take her mind off her stomach she racked her brains for any useful information she might have acquired about cauterising wounds. Burning with hot tar, she recalled. Well, that was helpful, she could just see Paget sitting still while she applied boiling pitch to his leg. Soldiers in the Peninsular Wars had bound maggots into an open wound, leaving them to eat away the bad flesh, she remembered reading somewhere, but even if she had known which maggots they used, odds were there weren't any round here, and again, she couldn't quite see Paget allowing her to do any such thing. Whisky? Raw spirit? Poultice? Pulling the medicine box towards her, she peered hopefully inside. There wasn't much bandage left either, although she supposed they could always resort to tearing up sheets. The antiseptic cream was really only for small cuts and insect bites. TCP? It would sting like hell, but would it actually help?

'Stop looking so worried,' he retorted from behind her. 'It gives me no confidence at all.' Hobbling round to sit beside her, he too peered into the box. 'What have we got?'

Rather too aware of his close proximity, she glanced at him. His hair was wet and a lone rivulet of water was running down the side of his face; before she could stop herself, she'd wiped it away.

'The leg, O'Malley,' he reminded her drily, his eyes laughing at her, and she flushed, then grinned ruefully.

'You shouldn't be so damned attractive, then,' she muttered, and he burst out laughing. It was so unfair, she thought, sighing; everything about him was attractive, his laugh, his voice, his body. An irresistible package, and she wondered fleetingly what his wife had been like. How long had she been dead? Did he miss her still?

'TCP, that'll do,' he muttered, drawing her attention back; taking the bottle from the box, he unscrewed the top.

'It'll hurt,' she warned, almost wincing in anticipation.

'It hurts now,' he murmured. Hitching up the towel that he was wearing knotted round his hips, he folded the other towel he was carrying and put it beneath his thigh. Taking a deep breath, he poured the contents of the bottle over the wound, and O'Malley gritted her teeth and shut her eyes tight, almost as though it were her own leg it was being poured on to. The short, panting breaths he was taking told their own story, and O'Malley cautiously peeped at him. His eyes were screwed shut, his head thrown back and the sinews in his throat stood out like cords. His hands were clenched round his thigh below the wound, but gradually, as she watched, the tension went out of him and he began taking normal breaths.

'Jesus! That'll teach me to play hero,' he breathed. Grimacing at her, he picked up the tube of antiseptic, 'Might as well go the whole hog, don't you think?' And, cutting off a large square of lint, he spread the contents of the tube on it before slapping it over the cut. 'Over to you, Florence,' he quipped, extending his leg across her knee for her to dress it.

Picking up the roll of bandage, she slowly and methodically wrapped it round his thigh. She felt exhausted, she'd never have made a nurse. 'When I get back,' she promised, 'I'm going to take a course in first aid. I feel so damned useless.'

'Not a feeling you're very used to, I imagine,' he smiled. 'Never mind, I've had worse and survived. And at least you didn't faint.'

'Is that supposed to comfort me?' she asked wryly.

Smiling again, he traced a gentle finger across her nose. 'Big brown eyes, like a spaniel. Is this your natural colour?' he asked, fingering a strand of her thick hair.

'Mm. Looks like a banana split ' she murmured ruefully.

'Unusual, and beautiful. Come on, give me a hand into the bedroom. I'll lie down for a bit, then perhaps Jenny will be awake and we can have something to eat.'

Getting to her feet, she put her arm round him and helped him hop towards the bedroom. 'Good job I'm a big girl,' she gasped as they lurched awkwardly to the bed. 'You're not exactly a lightweight, you know. How tall are you?'

'Six four—just the right height for you, O'Malley,' he remarked on a thread of laughter. Throwing himself on to the bed, he dragged her down after him then rolled on top of her.

'Mind your leg!' she exclaimed breathlessly and somewhat automatically, because the green eyes staring down into her own gradually shut out all other thoughts and concerns entirely, and warmth spread through her lower abdomen as dark lashes flickered and closed and his mouth descended to warmly cover hers.

The kiss was slow, almost drugged, as their lips clung, reluctant to part, and as he grazed his mouth across her cheek to her ear he husked softly, 'This what you want, O'Malley?'

'Yes,' she whispered equally softly, unable to lie as her arms went round him. 'You know it—I know it, why pretend? Although in my own defence, may I just point out that this is not how I normally behave?'

'You can point out any damned thing you please,' he muttered as he tongue traced the perfect pattern of her inner ear and she grunted with exasperated laughter. Leaning up, he stared down into her face. He was smiling widely. 'O'Malley, I . . .'

'Daddy?'

The sad little cry could hardly be ignored, and O'Malley sighed, then smiled ruefully as Paget gave a snort of amusement and rolled on to his back, his arms spread wide. 'Foiled again.'

'I'll see to her,' she said, climbing to her feet. 'You get some rest.' As she reached the door, she turned to stare back at him, then grinned naughtily. 'Who would have thought it would be so damned difficult to get seduced?'

Closing the door, she heard him chuckle. Her own mouth curving in a smile, she walked to the sofa. Leaning her arms along the back, she smiled down at Jenny.

'Hi, have a nice sleep?'

Eyes that were so like her father's stared up at her, confusion and almost fear in their depths. 'Where's Daddy?' she asked worriedly.

'He's lying down, resting his leg. Truly,' she insisted as Jenny continued to look worried. 'Why not go and see? I'll see what we can have for dinner.'

Scrambling off the sofa, Jenny walked warily towards the bedroom. Giving O'Malley an odd look over her shoulder, she slowly pushed the door wide and disappeared inside. Frowning, O'Malley went into the kitchen to investigate the cupboards. Why was she so afraid? Of what? It was almost as if she expected her father to suddenly disappear. Had he before, when Jenny was younger? Shaking her head, knowing she wouldn't get any answers unless Paget chose to volunteer the information, she dragged the bag of potatoes over to the sink and began peeling.

She gave them corned beef, mash and tinned peas. There was plenty of tinned stuff, two big sacks of potatoes, a box of oranges, endless tins of milk and a sack of sugar. They wouldn't starve, that was for sure, but why so much? How long was Paget intending to stay here for goodness' sake? Months? What about Jenny's schooling? She impatiently pushed the thoughts away; speculation was useless. She had also expected that Stavros would have been back by now, but when she enquired all she got was a smile and a shrug.

Paget unearthed a pack of cards and they spent the evening playing snap, followed by pontoon and then poker. Jenny was quick to learn and, for the first time since she'd met her, O'Malley heard her laugh. She wondered at the swift stab of pain that crossed Paget's face. He seemed to watch his daughter with a sort of hunger, yet when he caught her looking at him his face resumed its bland expression. He was a total enigma. Confusing, irritating, and wildly attractive. Considering she had done very little all day, by nine o'clock she felt exhausted. Borrowing another of Paget's shirts, she rinsed out her underwear and the one she had been wearing all day, plus Jenny's and Paget's things. There was a rope, she remembered, in the broom cupboard; fixing a line up outside, she hung out the washing. So long as the wind didn't get up in the night, it should be all right. When she went back inside, Paget was idly building a card house.

'Jenny gone to bed?' she asked, coming to stand behind him.

'Mm.' Then he muttered crossly as the pile of cards collapsed. Shuffling them together, he put them back in the box and leaning back in his chair he stretched widely. 'You might as well do the same,' he murmured, getting stiffly to his feet. 'I'm going for a walk around.'

'Bored, Paget?' she taunted, a gleam of amusement in her eyes. 'You should learn to relax.'

His mouth twisted wryly, and he slapped her rear before walking out. Staring after him, she heaved a sigh. Her company wasn't required, that was obvious. A subtle hint that Paget preferred to do his own chasing? Well, she wasn't daft enough to need telling twice. It was galling, all the same. Sitting in the chair he had just vacated, she emptied out the cards and began her own structure. What had he been going to say before Jenny had woken up? 'O'Malley, I . . .' I what? The fact that he wanted to be by himself now that there was an opportunity to resume where they had left off could only lead her to suppose that it hadn't been I want you, I want to make love to you, or even, I like you. Absently adding cards to the growing pile, her eyes were blank as her thoughts revolved uselessly. It was becoming increasingly important to her that she know all about him. His name, what he did, why he was there—how he felt about her. With an irritable little gesture, she knocked the card house down; it rather smacked of building castles in the air. As he'd said, she might as well go to bed. She'd made her feelings very clear, now it was up to him, and on that unsatisfactory thought she went to clean her teeth. She didn't think Jenny would mind that she used her Mickey Mouse toothbrush.

* * *

She must have been tireder than she thought, because she didn't hear Paget come to bed, and when she woke in the morning she was alone. There was a strange thudding noise coming from outside, followed by childish laughter, and she knelt up on the bed to peer from the window. Paget was hammering pieces of wood into the ground, and she frowned in puzzlement until she realised what it was he was making. A wicket. Oh goody, she thought waspishly, they're going to play cricket.

When she'd washed and collected the dry garments from the makeshift line, she breakfasted on stale bread and jam. Surely Stavros should have been back by now? she thought worriedly. Yet there'd been no sign of the truck outside.

Wandering outside, she watched Paget instruct his daughter in the art of cricket. The bat was a flat piece of firewood with a piece of rag tied round the end as a handle. The stumps were also firewood, she saw, the ball was a rock. Wonderful. As she watched, the makeshift ball made a slow arc towards Jenny who, with a look of determination on her face, draw back the bat and whacked it for all she was worth. The bat cracked in half and the ball whizzed past O'Malley's ear with inches to spare.

'I do realise I'm an unwanted guest,' she murmured with an edge of sarcasm, 'but is it quite necessary to kill me?'

'Don't exaggerate, O'Malley,' Paget said, grinning as he limped towards her, 'it missed you by a mile. However, now that you are here, we need a fielder. It will relieve the boredom,' he teased softly as he halted in front of her. 'Good morning,' he added, bending his head to kiss her gently on the lips. 'May I say how entirely delightful you look?'

'You may,' she said, suddenly restored to good humour. 'You may also tell me where the hell Stavros is!'

'He'll be here,' he murmured, giving her arm a little pat that she supposed was meant to be comforting. Then, holding up the broken stick, he explained solemnly, 'I have to get a new bat.' Moving round her, he went to rummage in the broom cupboard. 'Get the ball, will you?'

Shaking her head ruefully, O'Malley went to retrieve the rock. With more enthusiasm than skill she fielded for Jenny, and as the girl whacked the rock above O'Malley's head she ran backwards in an effort to catch it and promptly fell over a boulder that she had forgotten was there. Winded, she lay for a few moments to try and get her breath back. Her eyes closed, she saw red whirls on the inside of her lids and she groaned. Hadn't her poor body taken enough punishment in the last few days?

'O'Malley?' Paget asked worriedly. As he knelt beside her, a gentle hand pushed the hair back off her forehead, and she was tempted for a moment to ham it up, but only for a moment. If Jenny hadn't been watching she might have done because it was very, very tempting. A bit of cosseting would have been very nice, but Jenny was there and she seemed to have more than enough worries on her young mind.

'I'm all right,' she breathed, opening her eyes.

'Just winded. It was my own silly fault for showing off.'

'Yes,' he murmured, a gleam of humour in his eyes.

'Would you like to bat, O'Malley?' Jenny asked shyly, proffering the stick.

'I would adore to bat,' she said, extending an arm to each of them to be pulled up. 'Unfortunately, I think my skill as a batsman only equals my skill as a fielder, and we'd probably wait an awful long time for me to score. I'll bowl, let your dad have a go.'

They played for another hour until it got too hot, then retreated indoors for some lunch, by which time Jenny had quite overcome her shyness and was behaving like any other five-year-old, laughing and boisterous, showing off slightly because she had scored more runs than her father. Paget too was more relaxed than she had ever seen him, his smile wider, the caution gone from his eyes—and wouldn't she just like to know what had put it there in the first place. When Jenny had fallen asleep, she and Paget remained seated at the table.

'Has she been ill?' she asked, and when he merely raised his eyebrows in query she explained, 'She seems to sleep a lot.' She could have kicked him when he shrugged. 'Not exactly forthcoming, are you?'

'No, O'Malley, I'm not.' Stretching his hands across the table to hers, he said seriously, 'I can't explain, not at the moment anyway, and to be honest, much as I like you, you're a distraction I really do not need. If I had any sense, I would have

left you when we first emerged from the ruins.'
Giving a rueful smile, he explained. 'You rather
took me by surprise. It's been a long time since I met
anyone who could make me smile. But I do thank
you for the way you've been with Jenny. She's not
been very used to—kindness or involvement.' And
his hesitation over the words only intrigued and
exasperated her further.

'Discounting you?' she probed gently.

Sighing, he leaned back in his chair and, his eyes
distant, he murmured, 'I couldn't always be there.'
Whichever particular fate it was that decreed they
would be interrupted, O'Malley wished to perdition.
Before she could ask him to explain, they both
heard the labouring engine of the truck. 'Stavros!'
he exclaimed, sounding relieved and O'Malley
stared at him curiously. Had he been worried, too?
As he got to his feet and walked outside to wait,
O'Malley slowly followed. As soon as Stavros
pulled up, he was out of the cab, and, with a wary
glance at O'Malley, motioned Paget to join him
away from her. Their muttered conversation seemed
to involve rather a lot of arm waving, and she
strained her ears to hear. Were they arguing? When
Paget eventually turned, his face was grim, and
whatever it was Stavros had told him it must have
had something to do with her because the look he
gave her would have stripped paint.

'Paget?' she murmured worriedly as he went to
walk past, her hand touching his arm.

'Don't touch me!' he gritted. 'Don't talk to me,
don't come anywhere near me—because the way I

feel right now I'm likely to strangle you!' And pushing rougly past he strode into the house.

Staring after him in astonishment, she suddenly hastened to catch him up. 'What in God's name is going on?' she demanded in bewilderment. 'You can't just make provocative statements and expect me to meekly agree without knowing the reason. Come on, Paget. If you have something to say, say it!'

'All right!' he snarled. 'I liked you, O'Malley! I thought you were different. Well, more fool me, because I should have known, shouldn't I? All the clues were there, being at the ruins at that particular time, the name that was no name, the questions . . .'

'What questions? What name?' she asked, bewildered. 'And you knew why I was at the ruins, I was meeting someone!'

'Yes! A damned photographer!'

Staring at him, at the rigid angry face, she felt her heart dip. 'How did you know he was a photographer?' she asked weakly. 'How, Paget? How?' she screamed when he didn't answer. Dear God, had Stavros come across Nick's body? Had someone in the village found him?

'A man was asking questions . . .'

'What man?' she demanded urgently, grabbing his arm and practically shaking it.

'How the hell should I know?' he shouted, wrenching himself free of her. Pushing her away, he slammed into the bedroom. Glancing after him, sickness and fear overriding every other emotion, she dashed outside and grabbed Stavros's arm.

'What man, Stavros? What man was asking questions? Answer me, damn you!' And maybe her fear was reflected on her face, because he didn't shrug away as Paget had done, he answered quite gently. 'His name was Nick . . .' And she swayed, shutting her eyes tight.

'He was all right?' she whispered.

'Yes. He was asking after you.'

'And you told him I was all right?'

'Yes,' he murmured after a short pause, and O'Malley stared at him in sudden suspicion. He'd sounded almost evasive.

'You did tell him?' she repeated, her body tense.

'Yes. Now if you'll excuse me—I have things to do.'

What things? she thought, blankly staring after him as he walked back to the truck. There was nothing round here to do! Striding after him, she demanded, 'Was the village all right? Is that where Nick's waiting?'

'No,' he muttered as he lifted the bonnet of the truck. Peering inside, he ignored her.

'Stavros!' she persisted, beginning to lose her temper. 'Where exactly was he?'

'On the road,' he mumbled without lifting his head. 'I had more important things on my mind. I told him I'd seen you and that you were all right. He said OK and that was it.'

'And the village was destroyed?'

'Yes.'

'Were many killed?'

'I don't know! I can't tell you anything else.'

Taking a spanner from his back pocket, he began tinkering with the engine, and every time she attempted another question he just banged louder. Paget, she thought mutinously. Paget had told him not to talk to her. Right. Whirling away from Stavros she stormed back inside. Something was going on, and she determined to find out just what it was! Shoving open the bedroom door, she came to a frustrated halt. Paget was sitting on the edge of the bed, watching his daughter. At her entrance he looked up, his eyes hard.

'You want to fight it out in here? Or outside?' she gritted. 'Personally, I don't give a damn!' She did, she had no desire to hurt Jenny further, which a fight with her father would certainly do, but she had no intention of telling him that, neither had she any intention of keeping quiet.

After a long, telling moment, he said tersely. 'Outside.'

Not bothering to make sure he followed, she led the way outside and round to the far side of the house where they weren't likely to wake Jenny with their shouting, because shouting there was certainly going to be. On her side, at any rate.

'Right,' she said crisply. Leaning back against the wall, she folded her arms across her chest. 'Let's have it. What the hell is going on?'

'Don't play games, O'Malley,' he grated, standing square in front of her. 'You know what the hell is going on—only you didn't expect me to find out, did you?'

'Find out what?' she demanded, and when he

didn't answer she gritted, 'If I have to drag every word out of you syllable by syllable, I'll do it, even if it takes all night! Now, what have you found out?'

'That you're a damned reporter?'

'And?' She demanded tersely, but her mind was whispering no, oh, no, please don't let it be him, only she knew that it was a wasted prayer. The only reason it could possibly matter that she was connected to the Press was because he was the property developer.

'And you and your boyfriend have been poking and prying into my affairs, asking questions! But, like all media types, you can't be honest, can you, can't ask straight out? No, all of you are devious, deceitful, and what you can't find out you make up.'

'No,' she said staunchly. 'Not me. I was only . . .'

'I know what you were only!' he yelled, making her jump, and thrusting his face close to hers he grated harshly, 'People like you make me sick! You prod and pry into poeple's lives, arrogantly assume you know what's best . . .'

'I do?' she exclaimed incredulously. 'My God, Paget, talk about the pot calling the kettle black! Aren't you just as guilty of the same thing?'

'No! Because I have a right!'

'Well, so do I!' she stormed furiously, refusing to back down. 'So does the public! And if I have to walk until I find some civilisation, then I'll bloody well walk! Because if you think I'm staying here,' she hissed, furious and hurt that it had all gone so horribly wrong, that Nick had embroiled her in his wretched plans, 'then I'm not! People like you don't deserve to get away with riding roughshod over everybody!'

'You're not going anywhere, O'Malley,' he said with soft menace, and she looked at him in astonishment. She was even more astonished when he placed one large palm either side of her against the wall, effectively trapping her. 'Until this is resolved, you are staying right here.'

'Oh, really?' she drawled sarcastically. 'Threats, Paget?'

'Believe it, O'Malley,' he said very softly, his words dropping like pebbles into a still pool. 'If I have to tie you up to prevent you leaving, then I will. Make no mistake, you are not leaving until I say so. There will be no little newspaper articles, no photographs, no nothing. And there will be only one winner. Me.'

'Want to bet?' she muttered, suddenly determined that come hell or high water she would not be intimidated by him, though it was fearsomely hard to hold his level stare.

'I don't think you've been listening, O'Malley,' he said, sounding almost conversational. 'I've gone too far to back down now—and if you really think you can take me on and win, then by all means try—I might even enjoy the fight.'

There was no even about it, it was patently obvious that he enjoyed a fight. Well, so did she, in moderation, only she had a horrible feeling moderation wasn't a word in his vocabulary, not where she was concerned anyway. However, never one to give in tamely, she pinned the most insolent look she could find on to her face, and drawled in fair replica of his own voice, 'You don't frighten me, Paget—and aren't you forgetting Nick?' she asked sweetly, her mouth curving into a mocking smile. 'You think he'll be content to wait around in the ruins of Sophia? When I don't turn up he'll come looking—and believe me, I'd pit Nick against you any day.'

'And why should—Nick—find you?' he asked, giving her father's name the nastiest inflexion he could find.

'Because Stavros told him where I was,' she said triumphantly.

'Did he?' he asked softly. 'Did he, O'Malley?'

'Yes!' she gritted.

Giving her a taunting smile that was far superior to her own meagre effort, he pushed himself upright. 'I think you may find you have a rather longer wait than anticipated for your white knight to rescue you.'

'Meaning?' she asked between her teeth.

'Meaning Stavros *didn't* tell him where you were.' And she was too stunned for a moment to answer. Her eyes locked with his, her mouth opening and closing like a landed fish, and he grinned nastily. 'I'll let you go in—oh, about a week, I should think,' he drawled.

'A week? Are you insane? You can't keep me locked up here for a week against my will!'

'Can't I? I can do any damned thing I please.

Something you would do well to remember.' And
when she erupted in temper, her fists swinging wildly,
he caught them easily in his large hands.

'Still want me, O'Malley?' he taunted—then
laughed, actually laughed as she tried to find his shins
with her feet. Then, as if bored, he tossed her hands
away from him, swivelled on his heel and walked
away. With a yell of fury, she launched herself at his
back and was never afterwards quite sure what
happened next. One moment she was hurling herself
at his arrogant back, and the next she was spread-
eagled flat on the hard, stony ground, Paget on top
of her. Dragging the ejected breath back into her
lungs, she fought to get free.

'Get off me!' she gritted. Never, ever in her entire
life had she been manhandled in such a way, and
temper darkened her eyes to black. 'Get off me,
Paget!'

'Why?' he gritted, his jaw like granite. 'You'd
have flattened me given half a chance, so why should
I behave differently? You're a leech, O'Malley, the
worst kind. You fasten on to other people's misery
for gain . . .'

'Are you insane?' she screeched, her chest heaving.
'I think that terminology applies to you! You're the
one causing pain! Overriding people's wishes and
needs for your own selfish ends—cheating and
stealing—yes, stealing!' she hissed. 'Did you take
their feelings into account? Did you even ask them
what they felt? No! You want, so you must have!
You . . .'

'Shut up!' he snarled. 'Just shut up, O'Malley!

You don't know anything about it.'

'Oh, don't I?' she stormed, fighting to get free. Somehow his feet had locked painfully across her ankles, his rock-hard chest was crushing her ribs and his hips were grinding painfully into her own. She could feel every damned rock and pebble beneath her, and every time she struggled she only succeeded in hurting herself more, but if he expected her to beg for mercy he was going to be disappointed, she'd die first. Dragging a deep breath into her poor squashed lungs, she grated, 'I know enough to know you've overridden everyone's feelings to get your own way.' She didn't in fact actually know anything of the sort, but if hurling insults was going to be a national pastime, then she was damned well going to qualify!

'And you're a model of rectitude, I suppose?' he spat. 'Not only a liar but . . .'

'When have I lied?' she demanded furiously.

'When you told me you were a damned nanny!'

'Ooh, ooh,' she floundered, momentarily lost for words, 'if that doesn't beat all! And that, that from a man who blatantly, without a flicker of an eyelid, told me he was writing a book! Don't talk to me about lying, Paget. Compared to you, I'm a mere novice.'

'Novice?' he yelled. 'You've never been a novice in your entire life! From the day you were born you probably twisted life to suit you, and you're worse than most of your breed, you trade on your looks!'

'I do not!'

With a look of contempt, he got to his feet. Stepping over her, he walked away.

CHAPTER FOUR

'BASTARD!' she spat. Easing herself carefully into a sitting position, she leaned weakly back against the wall. She felt bruised and exhausted, her mind numb. It was hard to believe the last few minutes had actually happened. One moment they had been sitting at the table having an amicable discussion—no, more than amicable—and now she was arch enemy number one. Her shoulders slumping tiredly, she stared at the distant mountains. The sky was darkening, turning to purple, and she felt suddenly lonely and confused. Oh, Nick, she thought, where are you? Are you thinking about me? Or am I relegated to the back of your mind now that you know I'm safe? Or did he know? Had Stavros lied about that, too? Feeling her eyes fill with tears, she lowered her head to her knees. She didn't want him to be a property developer, she thought bleakly. She would far rather he be a smuggler or a criminal. Rubbing her hands absently down the backs of her legs to dislodge the dust and gravel, she lifted her head to stare round her. So inhospitable, so bleak, and she felt bitter disappointment fill her. She'd liked him, as he had confessed he'd liked her. She thought, stupidly as it happened, that she'd found a man to match up to Nick, but a man who could despoil a lovely stretch of coastline for material gain, a man who could override the opinion of the locals, wasn't the man for her. Even if he had wanted her, had not found out about herself and Nick, she could not love a man who gave no thought to others.

Nick had said the property developer was hard, selfish and arrogant, even though he had not personally met him, and he was that and more because he didn't seem to consider he was in the wrong. Why? she wondered. What drove a man like that? Neither she nor Nick had ever wanted money, or only enough to live on, for their needs—and that's because you've never been without it, O'Malley, she told herself disgustedly. When have you ever gone hungry? When have you been unable to pay the rent? You've never known the indignity of the dole queue. Had Paget? Was that what drove him? Made him so determined that the deal would go through? For himself and his daughter? And how had he known that Nick was a photographer? Or that they were interested in the same strip of land? Frowning, she got to her feet and went inside; she really did need to know that, because maybe, just maybe they had got their wires crossed.

Paget was lying on the sofa, idly turning the pages of a book that was resting on his chest. He looked totally unconcerned. No one looking at him now would guess at the turmoil he had generated such a short time ago. And the fact that she had turned out to be something other than he'd suspected didn't seem to bother him either, and that made her angry all over again.

'How did you know Nick was a photographer?' she demanded bluntly, coming to stand by his feet.

Giving a long, exasperated sigh, he lowered the book. 'He could hardly be anything else with his neck hung about with expensive equipment, zoom lenses and the like—could he?' he sneered disparagingly.

'He could be a tourist.'

'Is he?' he asked, his eyes hard.

'No,' she mumbled, unable to lie.

'No,' he said flatly. 'No more than you're a nanny.'

'It doesn't necessarily follow that I'm working with him . . .' Then she winced as the book was flung across the room to land with a crash against the far wall.

'No, it doesn't necessarily follow,' he grated. Getting awkwardly to his feet, he walked into the bedroom and shut the door.

Staring after him, she sighed drearily. So, that was that. *Finito*. No point in staying, then, was there? No. Determination firming her jaw, she marched back outside. The truck was still standing out front, of Stavros there was no sign. Walking across to it, trying to make her actions casual in case Stavros was watching, she walked all round it, and when nothing happened, no shouts or dire warnings, she hastened up into the cab and pulled the starter. Nothing. Swearing, scraping her knuckles on the dashboard in her haste, she tried again. Nothing, not even the sound of the motor trying to turn. Damn, that was what Stavros had been up to, disabling the blasted engine. Climbing down, she slammed the door, then aimed a childish kick at the tyres. All right, she'd walk. If it took days, she'd walk and to hell with them. Whirling round, she set off in the direction of the track. It presumably went somewhere, there would have been no point in it being there otherwise. Once out of sight of the house she felt more confident. Hah. Can't leave, eh? You just watch me, Paget whatever-your-name-is. You just watch.

So intent on the imaginary conversations she was holding in her head, and the hurt and disappointment she was feeling, she didn't at first hear the engine labouring somewhere behind her. When she did hear it, it was too late, the twin pale beams of the headlights were already rounding the curve. Halting in shock, she glanced frantically round, searching for an escape route, then darted into the rocks beside the track and wasted a lot of unnecessary energy scrambling upwards, only to be hauled unceremoniously back by Paget's brutal grip on the back of her shirt.

'Oh, no,' he gritted, swinging her round to face him. 'In the truck, O'Malley.' When she didn't immediately obey, just stared at him mutinously, her lovely eyes dark with temper, he picked her up and tossed her over his shoulder. He totally ignored her pummelling fists against his back, and when he reached the truck he dumped her in the passenger seat. 'I told you, O'Malley, you aren't going anywhere until I say so.'

'Go to hell!' she muttered rebelliously. Folding her arms across her chest, she stared resolutely out of her window as Paget climbed in beside her. She knew the

sheer futility of trying to outrun him. Even with a
bad leg he would catch her, she knew that. Well,
there was more than one way to skin a cat—she just
had to think of it, that was all. Jenny was the
stumbling block; it it hadn't been for her, she could
have been as ruthless as Paget. Well, nearly, she
qualified to herself. She could maybe have knocked
them both out, tied them up . . . Then she gave a
dreary little laugh. She could no more wallop him
over the head than fly. Stealing a glance at his set
face, she wondered if the same rules would apply to
him. Would he hit her over the head if the need
arose? Probably, but he'd be careful not to start
anything in front of his daughter, wouldn't he? Yes,
she thought, he probably would. Unfortunately, she
wasn't unprincipled enough to upset Jenny, either.
Looking at him, it was hard to believe that he had
any other facet to his character than the one he was
displaying now. He looked like a tough, ruthless
mercenary, she decided, his earlier humour and
gentleness might never have been.

'Why?' she asked as they rolled to a stop in front
of the house. 'Why is it so damned important that
you win?'

As he pulled the handbrake on with a vicious jerk
of his wrist, she flinched; there was a cold savagery
about him that was frightening. For two pins, she
thought, he might just strangle her.

'Why?' he grated, his face thrust close to hers, his
eyes pinning her in her seat. 'Why? Dear God, but
you play it out to the bitter end, don't you,
O'Malley? If I hadn't found out about your precious

Nick, I'd have swallowed it all whole, wouldn't I? You acted your part very well, I'll give you that.' His face registering his disgust for his own gullibility, he swung away and climbed down. He no longer limped, she noticed absently, her brows pulled into a frown as she digested his odd remarks; it was as though he now had no time for such mundane things as injuries. Then, suddenly realising what he had been implying, she swung herself down and hastened after him; it was only later she castigated herself for her stupidity. In his anger with her he'd forgotten to disable the truck, and she could have driven off; neither would have been able to catch her on foot. Only she was too full of anger to think straight; she was only intent on catching him. Grabbing his arm as he was about to push inside, she hung on grimly until he turned.

'If you honestly think I behaved as I did to get round you, get information, then I pity you! I pity you for your cynicism, for your lousy judge of character—because let me tell you Mr High-and-bloody-mighty Paget, I'd sell myself for no man—let alone a damned shark like you! And,' she hissed breathlessly, 'if that's the opinion you have, then I'll have no compunction in behaving as you seem to think I already have! Be warned, Paget, I won't submit meekly to being kidnapped! I'll use any means I can to get free!' Brave words of defiance, but she was damned if she was going to let him trample all over her.

If she thought he'd looked menacing before, she was wrong. Before he'd looked like a mere pussy-cat

compared to how he looked now, and she took a
hasty step backwards, her eyes wary. He followed as
she retreated until she was pressed up against the
truck, his face a cold mask of fury.

'You do anything, any—damned—thing—to hurt
or upset Jenny, so help me, O'Malley, I'll kill you.
Do you understand? Do you understand?' he
growled, one hand lifting. Convinced he was going to
hit her, she got in first and swung her fist in a wild arc
that unexpectedly connected with his jaw. Not that
her puny defence had any effect other than to make
him madder than he already was.

'Don't you hit me, Paget!' she screeched, dodging
to one side. Then she gasped in shock as he caught
her arm and slammed her back against the truck so
hard that her teeth rattled.

'Your word, O'Malley,' he breathed softly, and
when he took a deep, slow breath and punishingly
increased the pressure on her upper arm she hastily
gave it.

'I give it. *I give it*!' she yelled as he increased the
pressure even further. Flinging her arm away from
him, he indicated that she now precede him into the
house.

Refusing to rub her sore arm while he was
watching, she flung her head back proudly and
marched inside. Jenny was now tucked up on the
sofa; presumably Stavros had moved her while Paget
chased after *her*.

'Bedroom,' he said succinctly.

Gritting her teeth, she walked into the bedroom.
Paget closed the door on her, and only then did she

let her pent-up breath out. Collapsing weakly on to the side of the bed in a shivering heap, she shakily examined her arm. Nice bruise she was going to have there! Angry red marks showed where his fingers had bitten, and her mouth tightened mutinously. If she had to dig her bloody way out, she would. Animal! Nothing in her life had prepared her for such violence, but instead of being frightened of it as any sane person would, she was actually revelling in the confrontation! My God, she must be mad. But, despite her nervous tension, there was also a tingling excitement, and she groaned. What on earth was the matter with her? Staring rather blankly round her, she gradually focused on the little oil-lamp that was burning on the dresser beside a bowl of water. Thoughtful, she muttered derisively. There was also a bucket in the corner, and she ground her teeth in fury. Intended to keep her locked up, did they? Well, she'd see about that! Marching across to the window, she flung back the curtain. Boards had been nailed across outside, she saw in disbelief. My God, didn't waste much time, did they? She had been gone from the house barely a half-hour in her bid for freedom. And oh, wasn't it just dandy that they'd actually had some spare old boards they could use. A gap of about an inch had thoughtfully been left in the centre, and she was flooded with such an intense, destructive anger that she hammered her fist futilely against the boards. Her eyes darting round the room, she searched for a tool to use, something to lever the boards loose. Only there wasn't anything. Unless she dismantled the bed. All right, she'd dismantle the bloody bed. Gripping the metal frame beneath the mattress, she flung it over on to its side, and as it crashed noisily the door was flung open.

'Get out!' she screeched. 'This is my prison, visitors aren't welcome!' For a moment, as he surveyed the mess she had made, she thought he was going to laugh. His lips defiantly twitched, only then he presumably remembered she was one of the dreaded Press fraternity and his mouth hardened again. Giving her a look of derision, he went out again.

She felt stupid, because, really, how was she to dismantle a bed that was bolted together when she had nothing to dismantle it with? Not even a nail-file. 'Oh, knickers!' she muttered. Heaving the bed back on to its feet, she flung herself down on top. She'd think of something tomorrow, at the moment she was too tired. She'd rest first, in the morning she might be feeling more inspirational. It was a matter of pride now to best him. Some way, somehow, she vowed she would get away. From liking him and wanting him, she now detested him. He was cold, arrogant, single-minded, ruthless. Never mind what had made him like that, there had been absolutely no need to abuse her. Those steel fingers might very well have broken her arm, snapped it like a twig. Well, no man, no matter who he was, no matter how tough, was going to get the better of her. You just wait, Paget thingummy, you just damned well wait!

It was late when she woke, no doubt due to her prison being boarded up, she thought mutinously, going to inspect the boards in daylight. It would take more than a small lever to shift those she saw. So, not the window. Well, there were other ways to get away. Sleeping pills to put in their coffee would have been nice; unfortunately, she didn't have any. Marching over to the door, she rattled the handle and found to her surprise that it opened. Feeling an absolute idiot, which didn't improve her temper, she marched out. Stavros was sitting at the table, and his eyes shifted awkwardly away from her as she glared at him.

'Kidnapping is a punishable offence,' she said flatly, walking across to him. 'I hope . . .'

'I kidnapped you, not Stavros,' Paget said coldly from behind her. 'There's hot water for a bath if you want one,' he continued in the same, arctic tone. 'Breakfast is whatever you choose.' Striding past her, he went into the bedroom and she heard him rummaging in the chest of drawers. Storming out into the kitchen, she went into the bathroom and slammed the door, only to be forced out again as she realised she would have nothing to change into. The shirt she was wearing was filthy, and she was damned if she was going to wear her underwear another day without washing it out. Paget was standing in the main room, one of his shirts dangling from one finger which he extended as she marched in. Snatching it from him, her mouth tight, she marched back into the bathroom. God, she hated him. Mockery had been lurking in those green eyes, and she had an overwhelming urge to rush out and wallop him. Taking a long, deep breath to calm herself down, she stripped off and climbed into the bath.

By the time she had washed, rinsed out her clothes and dressed in the clean shirt, her temper had hardened into cool determination. She would have something to eat, then calmly and clear-headedly plan what she would do. It was absolutely no good going off half cocked. Careful planning and forethought was what was needed. She would be coolly polite to them both, treat Jenny much as she had always done. She would not give Paget the satisfaction of letting him see that he could rattle her.

Fine words. Unfortunately Paget's total indifference to her behaviour severely tested her resolutions to their absolute limit. One day had never seemed so long. Both men comprehensively ignored her, but wherever she went one or the other was always lurking nearby. Jenny looked bewildered, and O'Malley's heart went out to her. For her sake, not for anyone else's, she reiterated firmly to herself, she would try to behave normally, so she played a game of cricket with her, taught her jacky five stones and even hopscotch. She ate with them, for the simple reason that Stavros cooked enough for her and it was daft to cut off her nose to spite her face when she was hungry, but it was an ordeal, all the same. Never had a tongue been so bitten, she thought crossly. All those words squashed together in her throat like some ludicrous traffic jam, words she could not utter, not with Jenny present anyway.

After lunch, leaving someone else to wash up, she went for a walk. Her back ramrod stiff with a crazy defiance, she marched in the direction of the hills, the fact that Stavros ambled along behind her she ignored. Was he as fit as Paget? Her lips pursed, a militant gleam in her lovely eyes, she put it to the test.

Lengthening her stride, she made it to the foot of the hills, then, without a backward glance, she began climbing. She climbed up, down, round, scrambled on all fours where two feet wouldn't get her, all the time edging in the general direction of Sophia. Hot, sweaty, dusty, her hands and knees grazed, only stupid pride forced her on and a determination to best at least one of them. Unfortunately, forced marches over uneven ground weren't something she was entirely used to. A leisurely amble along Oxford Street was about her mark. After an hour, she gave up in disgust. Sitting on the nearest flat boulder, she looked behind her. Stavros was fit. He didn't look in the least distressed. His breathing was even, his face as calm as when he had set out. Picking up a rock, she threw it half-heartedly at him. To give him his due, he didn't look in the least triumphant, not how Paget would have looked anyway; he just looked miserable. Glaring disagreeably at him, she suddenly saw the funny side of it, saw how utterly ridiculous she must look, and she laughed, a warm rich, infectious chuckle. Give up, O'Malley. You ain't going to beat them, and at the rate you're going you'll only hurt yourself trying. It had never been Nick's intention that they do battle with the property developer, only that they report the facts. There wasn't even any great urgency about it; she could write up her notes when she got back, a few days either way wouldn't matter in the least.

Getting slowly to her feet, she groaned, her back

was killing her. Lurching over to where Stavros still stood, a wary, puzzled look on his face, she grinned. 'Come along, Stavros, old buddy, else we'll be late for tea.' Tucking her hand into his arm, she turned him in the direction of the house and promptly twisted her ankle on a loose stone. Sitting rather more abruptly than she had intended, she stared up at him through a wild tangle of hair. 'There is also a very strong possibility that you are going to have to carry me,' she said ruefully.

He didn't actually carry her, but he had to give her quite a bit of assistance. By the time the house came into sight she was more than regretting her impulsive behaviour. Paget was standing in the doorway, arms folded across his chest, his eyes narrowed as he watched her limp towards him.

'I know, don't say it,' she quipped breathlessly. 'I am stupid and thoughtless, but when all is said and done, I am the one who suffered. No one else. Now, if you will kindly move, I would like very much to sit down.'

A sardonic look on his face, he stepped to one side, and she hopped into the living-room and collapsed on the sofa. Jenny was sitting at the table playing with the cards, and she gave O'Malley a worried look.

'Hi,' O'Malley grinned. 'In future I'll leave mountain climbing to the goats. I don't suppose you would care to pour me a glass of orange, would you?' She smiled warmly as Jenny hopped down from the table and went into the kitchen. 'That's what I like,' she murmured, 'instant service.'

She could hear the two men's voices outside still, Stavros no doubt updating Paget on her behaviour, and she closed her eyes tiredly. She'd get up in a minute, have a bath, wash her hair. She was just drifting pleasurably, her limbs relaxed, when a cool, damp cloth was wiped gently across her hot face.

'Mm,' she mumbled sleepily, quite forgetting for a moment where she was. As her hands were wiped, she gave a faint smile; it was like being a little girl again, hands and face wiped before tea. As her sore ankle was gently grasped, she lifted weighted lids. Paget was perched on the end of the sofa, her ankle across his knee, a bowl of water on the floor beside him. Dark silky lashes hid his eyes, the soft dark hair had fallen across his forehead, and his carved face held a look of concentration as he carefully probed her ankle.

'I didn't know you cared,' she mumbled.

Turning his head he stared at her, the green eyes cold. 'I don't,' he said flatly. 'But if we have to leave here suddenly, I want you mobile, not holding everyone up because you have a bad ankle.'

'Ah,' she murmured. 'Silly of me. And is there a likelihood of us leaving here suddenly?'

'I just said so, didn't I?'

'So you did.' As he returned his attention to her ankle, she watched him. I could have fallen in love with you, she told him silently, and to her chagrin her eyes filled with tears. He wasn't watching her, yet he seemed to know and he turned his head.

'I'm hurting you?'

'Yes. A bit,' she said huskily. Not my ankle, but

my heart and my mind, my vision that I had of you,
us. But there had never been an us, that had only ever
been in her mind. Sighing, she said quietly, 'It's all
right, I just wrenched it a bit, I expect.' Nodding
indifferently, he got to his feet and she saw that
Jenny had been standing behind him, her orange
juice held carefully in her hands.

'Thanks, Jenny, you're an angel,' she said,
summoning up a smile. Taking it from the girl, she
took a long drink then hoisted herself into a sitting
position. As father and daughter went back to the
table, she found her eyes drawn to them. With his
daughter, Paget was gentle and patient, and she felt a
lump form in her throat. Why couldn't it have been
different? There was an ache inside her for this man
whom she had liked too much and who had turned
out to be so different from her hopes. Yet there was a
niggling feeling inside her that she had missed
something, some clue, because all the bits and pieces
didn't seem to add up. Her face pensive, she chewed
the inside of her lip, quite unaware that she was
doing so. He was a paradox, that was what he was.
She saw the pieces, could sometimes pick out the
feelings, and she would have sworn her instincts
about him when they had been in the ruins were
correct. He had been gentle, humorous,
teasing—wary, tense sometimes, but sort of
complete. Was that how he should have been? Before
something made him different? Made him act against
his nature? She was usually a very good judge of
character, and would have sworn that her reading of
him was correct. Yet her father had said the

property developer was ruthless, cold, uncaring of anyone but his own goals—and she just wished she could remember his name! Nick had told it to her, she knew he had, before he'd dropped her at the taxi rank in Alanya and gone off up the coast to take photographs. But she couldn't for the life of her remember what it was. She'd been too interested in what had been going on around her, she thought ruefully. Well, that would teach her to pay attention. Perhaps Nick had been wrong, his reading of the man had only been hearsay, after all.

'I've run you a hot bath, O'Malley,' Stavros said gruffly from the doorway, and she blinked in surprise and came back to the present. Giving him a warm, natural smile, she levered herself painfully upright. 'Thanks, Stavros. I didn't deserve that, did I? Not after dragging you over half of Turkey.' As she limped past him, she said teasingly, 'I'm going to go on a survival course when I get back, then we'll see who needs the assistance.'

Giving a grunt of laughter, he stared at her with a regretful look in his blue eyes.

'Don't,' Paget said, startling them both, and O'Malley stuck her tongue out at his back. He hadn't been talking to Jenny, that was for sure, and he must have damned good hearing if he had overheard her remarks. Must have eyes in the back of his head, too, if he'd picked up Stavros's regret. Giving a very unladylike snort, she went into the bathroom and closed the door.

At the rate she was going, her underwear was going to fall to bits before she could get back to

civilisation. Hooking it over the catch on the tiny
window to dry, she gave a wry grin. Well, that should
be interesting. Perhaps she could wear a pair of
Paget's pants? Gurgling with laughter, she climbed
into the bath. With a sigh of relief she leaned her
head back into the water.

When she returned to the living-room, her wet hair
combed back, her face shiny, she saw that Stavros
had laid the table for tea. Smoothing the worst of the
creases out of the shirt she had washed that morning,
she took her place. Mash and beans, tinned peaches
for afters, followed by strong black coffee.

'Where will Jenny sleep?' she asked of no one in
particular as she remembered that she was about to
be re-incarcerated in the bedroom for the night.

'I sleep on the sofa,' Jenny informed her shyly.
'Daddy sleeps in the chair . . .'

'And Stavros sleeps in the truck,' Paget put in.

'Oh, goody,' murmured O'Malley, giving him a
sweet smile. 'What time do all we good little children
go to bed?' she asked nicely, then grinned
unrepentantly as Stavros choked.

'You surely do like playing with fire, don't you,
sweetheart?' Paget drawled, sounding like something
from a B-movie.

'No, sir, I'm just naturally sassy,' she murmured
in a mock southern accent that she swore almost
made him smile.

'Bored already with the role of Amazon
O'Malley?' he asked insultingly as he leaned back in
his chair.

'To be totally honest, yes,' she replied, giving him

a look from under her lashes. 'It's so very exhausting. I thought I might try the meek female bit, see how that works.'

'It won't.' Tilting his chair back to the floor with a little thud, he got to his feet. Ruffling Jenny's hair, he announced. 'Bed.'

When they'd both gone into the bathroom, she turned a determined look on Stavros, who was looking decidedly wary. 'Don't,' he said, much in imitation of Paget earlier.

'Been told not to talk to the enemy?'

'I didn't need to be told, O'Malley,' he said gently before getting to his feet and beginning to clear the table. With a wry smile, she got up to help him.

'You don't need to——' he began.

'I know, and if I had any sense I wouldn't, but clearing the table is at least something to do. Idle hands and all that,' she teased. Looking at him curiously as they washed up, she asked, 'Were you really not in the least tired?'

'No.' And for a moment he looked as though he would say more, but caution obviously got the better of him, because he sighed and returned his attention to the dirty dishes.

Absently drying the plate she was holding, she went to stand at the open back door to stare up at the night sky. 'I'm not so bad, Stavros,' she said softly. 'Not as bad as he seems to think, anyway. I wish . . .' What? What did she wish? That he could be anything but a property developer? But he *was* a property developer, so it was foolish to wish, even on a star. They were truly beautiful out here, big and bright

and somehow comforting. 'Be nice if you could wish
yourself anywhere and be there, wouldn't it?' she
asked on a sigh. 'Just close your eyes, and when you
opened them, you were anywhere you chose. That
big bright star over there, maybe—although with my
luck, when I got there it would have died years ago
and all I would find would be a black hole.' Smiling
wryly, she turned and her eyes widened in surprise.
Paget was leaning back against the sink, his arms
folded. Stavros had gone.

'Gone out to check the truck,' he said laconically.

'Oh. I was just looking at the stars,' she said
lamely. For some silly reason, she felt embarrassed.
He was watching her so steadily, his face
expressionless. Had he heard her words about
herself? Well, she didn't care if he had, she thought
with a mental shrug. She wasn't so bad. 'Did
you . . .'

'Yes.' And she knew he knew to what she was
referring. She didn't know how she knew, but she
did.

'How bad are you, Paget?' she asked softly, her
eyes still locked with his, her hand still absently
drying the plate.

'Very bad.'

'Why can't I believe that?' she asked sadly. 'Why
can't I believe that you're all the things I know you to
be?'

'And why can't you be all the things I thought you
were?' he parried.

'I am. I never played the part you accused me of.
That was me. I . . .' His derisory smile locked the rest

of her words in her throat, and she looked away. When he unfolded his arms and moved towards her, she swallowed hastily. He removed the tea towel and plate from her lax hands and put them on the draining board. With one long finger he tilted her chin up so that she was forced to look at him. He had such beautiful eyes, she thought, so deep and clear, so green. The nose was aquiline, inviting the touch of her finger to trace its arrogant length. Her breath jerking unevenly, she stared up at him almost hypnotised. She wanted to brush the strands of hair from his forehead, smooth her palm across the silky stubble on his chin which she supposed vaguely could almost now be called a beard. His grey shirt was open to half-way down his chest, and she wanted to press her mouth to that strong column of throat. She should hate herself for wanting a man she should despise, and she had to forcibly remind herself that he was going to despoil lovely countryside. Build a holiday complex—create jobs, her mind whispered, create wealth. Was it so terrible? Loyalty to Nick should make her say yes, but the way he made her feel, just by watching her, not even touching her, sent loyalty spinning out of the window and her hands moved to lie flat against his strong chest.

He had abused her, called her names, hurt her, and none of it mattered a damn. What sort of person was she, for goodness' sake, that she could have so little pride? Dragging her eyes from his, she stared at his mouth. She wanted him to kiss her, and the most awful ache filled her so that she almost groaned aloud.

'Paget?' she whispered, returning her eyes to his.

'Yes, O'Malley?'

'I wish it could have been different.'

'Yes. I dare say you do.' With an impatient sigh, he asked coolly, 'Are you going to stand there all night?'

'What?' she asked, confused.

'I was waiting to pass,' he said with cruel mockery. 'Why else do you think I was standing here? To seduce you? Kiss you? Make love to you?'

'Oh, damn you!' she whispered, very near to tears. 'Damn you, you're all heart, aren't you? You keep me here against my will, give no thought to Nick, who's no doubt worrying himself to death about me, and all you want to do is pass. Well, you pass, Paget,' she gritted through a throat blocked with tears, 'you just keep on going till you get to hell!'

'Oh, don't talk to me about heart, O'Malley!' he said with sudden savagery. 'Because you have precious little of that commodity! And if you're so worried about your *friend*,' he sneered, 'write him a bloody note!' Turning his back, he began to walk out.

'Oh, very funny!' she yelled after him. 'What should I put? "Have been kidnapped by the property developer—abandon all plans to stop him and you can have me back?" Well, that's really likely to give him comfort, isn't it?'

He was so still that she thought for a moment he wasn't going to answer but just keep on walking, and then he turned, very, very slowly. If there was ever a man with murder in his heart, then she was staring at him. 'Property developer?' he asked softly, oh, so very softly.

'Yes,' she whispered, taking a hasty step backwards, just in case. Then, tilting her head defiantly, she said more firmly, 'Yes. Property developer! A man with so much heart that he can ruthlessly despoil a lovely stretch of countryside for gain! Who can milk profits from peasants just so he can wear designer jeans! Ride in fancy cars! Have a yacht, no doubt! Well, if you think Nick will give up just because you've kidnapped his . . .'

'Designer jeans?' he questioned, interrupting her tirade. 'Well, well, well, I forgot all about the designer jeans.' Giving her a look of scorn, he turned and walked out, and she stared after him in bewilderment. What had all that been about? In a burst of frustration and temper, she picked up a saucepan and hurled it after him.

Whirling round, she stalked back to the bedroom. Leaning back against the door, she glared at the oil-lamp, seeing only his face, hearing his taunts. Think I wanted to seduce you? Kiss you? 'No, I bloody didn't!' she yelled. Wanted him? Liked him? Dear God, she must have been out of her skull. Nick had been right, he was cruel—and you laid yourself wide open to that one, O'Malley, she told herself fiercely. Really asked for it. Well, you got what you deserved, perhaps now you'll have some sense. Pushing herself away from the door, her face set, she got ready for bed.

When she woke in the morning, they'd gone. She didn't need to search the house, she knew from the

complete silence that it was empty—a silence so
complete that it was deafening—and she felt
abandoned, hurt. A note was propped on the table
and, reaching out a shaky hand, she picked it up.

'The truck has sufficient fuel to get you to
Sophia, simply follow the road.'

When had they gone? And where? Without
transport, where could they go? Unless someone
came for them in the night? They must have moved
very quietly, or surely she would have woken.
Whirling round, she went back into the bedroom and
tugged open the drawers of the dresser. Clothes were
still neatly folded inside. In the top drawer were
Paget's shirts, shorts, a pair of jeans and underwear,
and she frowned. Why hadn't they taken them with
them? Because they would have woken her?
Smoothing her hand absently over the denim shirt
folded on top, she suddenly stopped. Above the top
pocket the name Paget was embroidered in red
cotton. Opening it fully, she looked at the label in the
back of the neck. Paget Shirts. And the memory of
the first time she had seen him flashed into her mind.
In the hotel, the receptionist's hand had been out
touching his chest. 'Paget,' she had said. Not his
name, of course not his name—she had been asking
about the label! No wonder he had looked amused
when she'd called him Paget. And then acceptance,
not correcting her, because he thought she knew his
real name—or no, he hadn't then, because he hadn't
known who she was. But later, when he'd found out
about Nick, he had put two and two together and

come up with five. He thought she had known his name all along, but because she was deceitful, playing a part, had called him Paget. Yes. That was it! Tossing the shirt angrily back into the drawer, she tugged open the bottom one. Jenny's things were lined up neatly inside and she frowned again. Everything looked new, unworn. In fact, some of the T-shirts were still in their cellophane wrappers. Rummaging quickly, she discovered that not one thing had been worn. Little canvas shoes still in their bag, socks still with the sticky tape holding them together. Underwear, jumpers, all new. Why? When you went away, you packed. Wherever you were going, you packed. Maybe not much, but something. A favourite teddy, a toy, but Jenny had had nothing. Why?

She had no idea how long she sat there trying to puzzle it out, and in the end she gave up. She simply did not know. Nor was she ever likely to find out now. Oh, well, she thought drearily, she might as well have a new shirt to drive into Sophia. Firmly pushing away thoughts of him, she made herself something to eat, then, filling two bottles with water and taking two packets of biscuits from the cupboard, she went out to the truck. It looked very forlorn standing there, a bit like she felt. She didn't like being on her own, she found, and that, from someone who often yearned for her own company, was ludicrous and she hated herself for her dependence on a man she should hate.

As far as the eye could see there was nothing. No animals, no birds, just a rocky landscape and an arc

of impossibly blue sky. Climbing into the truck, she
pulled the starter and visibly jumped; she'd forgotten
how noisy it was, it seemed to shatter the stillness,
reverberate from the mountains, rolls of sound that
deafened her. Putting it in gear, she drove cautiously
at first, struggling to hold the heavy vehicle on the
track, but as she gained confidence she increased her
speed and found to her surprise that it actually
handled better. After about half an hour, the road
forked, a dusty track led off to the right, and on
impulse she turned on to it. Ten minutes' driving
brought her to the coast and her lips tightened
angrily. Not walkable, eh? Hah! No more than half a
mile away were the ruins. He must have directed her
back and forth across the same track the night they
drove to the house, and she cursed herself for being
so stupid as not to notice. But why? He hadn't
known then about her connection with the Press. But
then she supposed that if he was hiding his interest in
the coastline he would hide it from everyone, not
only newspaper reporters. Not that the knowledge
made it any easier to bear.

The nearness of the ruins to the house also
answered another question that had been bugging
her. They must have had a boat, that was the only
explanation. They wouldn't have walked to the hills,
not with Jenny they wouldn't, so it had to be the
coast. Shading her eyes, she stared out to sea.
Nothing out there now, but she bet that was what
they had done. Was that why Paget had been at the
ruins? Waiting for a boat to pick them up? Well, it
hardly mattered now, they had gone and that was

that, but it was galling all the same; if she had used some gumption she could have left days ago. And would you really have wanted to? she asked herself. Angry that her thoughts kept reverting back to him, she stared at the crater left by the earthquake. It stopped about twenty yards short of the track she was on, but it would have been possible, if one walked carefully, to climb along the edge of the cliff. So if she had managed to get to the ruins, she wouldn't have been trapped, and the road she had travelled along by taxi the day of the earthquake was still intact. Sighing, she put the truck in gear.

As she negotiated the hill down into the village, she braked to a startled halt. Sophia lay spread out below her, unchanged, no sign of damage at all. 'Oh, you bastard!' she whispered. All that worry, all that anguish, for nothing. There was no sign of any earthquake. The village lay basking in the sunshine as it had always basked. The whitewashed villas, the profusion of flowers that everyone so loved, the sea a bright, sparkling blue lapping the rocky shore. Fishing-boats tugged playfully at their moorings, dipping and bobbing with the swell. Why? Why had they told her it was destroyed? What possible reason could they have had? Surely it would have been sufficient to tell her that the road was out? It explained Stavros's evasive behaviour, though. Oh, yes, it clearly explained that. Fool, she castigated herself. Fool.

Hot and sweaty, her arms and shoulders aching from wrestling with the truck, she drove the remaining distance to the village. Curious glances were thrown her way as she negotiated the narrow streets to the hotel, glances she did her best to ignore. Climbing wearily down, her shirt dusty and creased, her hair matted damply at her temples, she pushed through the bead curtain into the cool foyer. Nick was the first person she saw; he was slumped wearily against the reception desk, and, as he turned, the sight of his dear, familiar face made her burst into tears.

His arms were hard and warm and comforting as he crushed her tight against him, her face pressed into his shoulder.

'O'Malley, O'Malley, O'Malley,' he kept murmuring, his voice reflecting the strain he had been under. 'Where in God's name have you been? I've been going out of my mind!'

Sniffing, she lifted her head and gave him a watery smile. 'Sorry, I was just so pleased to see you.'

'But where have you been?' he asked incredulously. 'And just look at you!' he exclaimed. 'You look like a refugee!'

'I am a refugee,' she muttered. 'I got caught in the earthquake, remember?'

'Earthquake? What earthquake?'

'What do you mean, what earthquake?' she demanded incredulously, staring at him as though he'd gone mad. 'The earthquake up the coast which nearly killed me!' And she watched in astonishment as Nick's face drained of colour.

'But they said it was a landslip, erosion, no one said anything about an earthquake,' he said faintly.

'Landslip?' she retorted. 'I'll give them bloody

landslip! It nearly killed me!'

'But all it did was demolish an old monastery . . .' he began, bewildered.

'Yes! And who was sheltering in it? Me, that's who!'

'Oh, dear God,' he whispered. 'Dear God. Oh, hell, O'Malley, I need a drink.'

'*You* need a drink?' she asked faintly. '*You* do?' The sudden release from tension and worry made her laugh, then bite down on her lip hard as she felt it begin to spiral out of control. Taking a deep breath, she held it for a moment until she felt more in command, then with a weak grin she tucked her hand in his arm. 'Come on, I need a bath. You can get the drinks sent up,' she ordered huskily.

CHAPTER FIVE

WHEN she'd bathed and washed her hair, Nick had a meal sent up for her and, while she ate, she told him all that had happened.

'But didn't someone tell you?' she asked, puzzled. 'Stavros said he'd seen you and explained.'

'Short, stocky chap, brown shaggy hair, unshaven?'

'Yes.'

'Yes,' he said grimly. 'And I'd very much like to meet him again. Told me you'd gone to Alanya.'

'Alanya?' she exclaimed in astonishment. 'Why on earth would I go to Alanya? You must have misunderstood.'

'No, I didn't! He sent me there on a wild-goose chase because it was in the opposite direction to the one you were in!'

'Oh,' she said lamely, knowing he was right. Then, her mouth tightened, she muttered, 'Bastards.'

'Quite! I'd like to get my hands on the pair of them Did they hurt you?'

'No. No, they didn't hurt me,' she murmured. Not physically, at any rate—only emotionally. Then, aware of her father's sharp glance, she added hastily, 'Ironic, isn't it?' Out of all the people I could have been stuck with, it had to be the damned

106

property developer!'

'That, my darling, is sod's law. Anyway, I doubt he'll ever be building anything on that stretch of coastline. The landslip effectively put paid to his plans without any help from us.'

'Then why hold me captive? He must have known it was no longer a viable proposition. He saw the crater that was left as well as I did.'

'Mm,' Nick murmured thoughtfully. 'Odd that. Still, it's over now. Come on,' he said in a rallying tone, 'get yourself dressed and I'll buy you a drink. You sure as hell look as though you could do with one. I'll come and collect you in a few minutes. And, O'Malley,' he said as he reached the door, turning once more to face her, 'did I tell you lately how much I love you?'

Smiling, because her tough, lovable father looked so embarrassed at having put it into words, she nodded. 'The feeling is more than reciprocated,' she said huskily, her throat tight. Staring at him, at the impossibly blue eyes that still reflected the pain and worry he had gone through, she thought she'd like to kill Paget.

Sitting with Nick in the bar, they both attracted more than their fair share of admiring glances. O'Malley, striking in a sea-green dress, her fair hair a bright contrast among so many dark-haired people, and Nick, in a blue shirt that brightened his eyes, which O'Malley had teasingly suggested he had worn for that very reason, and his own light hair, more gold than fair, brushed neatly. She grinned, lifting her glass in a toast.

'You never did tell me why you weren't at the ruins to meet me,' she reminded him, and he stared at her in open-mouthed astonishment.

'Me?' he exclaimed ungrammatically. 'It was you who wasn't there! I waited for over an hour!'

Staring at him until his eyes shifted guiltily away, she asked softly, 'Which hour, Nick?'

'It wasn't so much which hour,' he mumbled, 'as which ruins.'

'Nick!'

'Well, I didn't realise until you told me you'd been in the ruined monastery that you'd been waiting at the wrong ruins.'

'*I* was waiting at the wrong ruins? *I* was?'

'Well, one of us was!' he exclaimed. 'I was at the one on the edge of town.'

'The fort!' she stated flatly. 'Nick, you distinctly told me the monastery.'

'Did I?' he asked innocently. Then, taking her empty glass, he asked airily, 'Another drink?'

Laughing, she shook her head at him. 'Wretch.'

When he returned, at his probing, she began to tell him of her adventures in more detail, and determinedly made her voice matter of fact. Nick was much too sharp to miss hesitations or nuances, and she wasn't ready to talk about her odd feelings for Paget, not yet anyway. She looked up curiously as the bead curtain into the bar rattled musically, and her eyes widened in astonishment. A tall, Nordic blonde had just come in, and as she paused rather dramatically in the entrance O'Malley grinned. Her face was made-up to perfection and her slim, almost thin body was clad in a tailored suit that looked extremely out of place in the noisy little bar. A twinkle in her lovely brown eyes, she murmured, *sotto voce*, 'Looks as though I have competition.' As her father turned his head curiously, he nearly choked on his drink.

'Oh, hell, the dreaded Evelyn.'

Staring at him in astonishment as he tried to look inconspicuous, she burst out laughing and nearly every head in the bar turned to look, smiles breaking out all round.

'Will you keep quiet?' he muttered.

'Been pursuing you, has she?' she murmured naughtily. If she had it was no wonder, her father was a very attractive man. Smiling affectionately at him, she teased, 'Not tempted, Nick?'

'Heaven forbid,' he muttered. 'She's not coming over, is she?'

'Not yet. She's still looking. Have you never wanted to marry again?' she asked curiously.

'No,' he said slowly, his face softening. 'Your mother was a hard act to follow. They don't seem to make them like that any more. You're a lot like her, you know. Not to look at, or only the eyes—it's a bit disconcerting sometimes to see her looking out at me. But your manner, your ways, that's Magda. Your humour and love of life. She was like a warm flame, she drew people to her, warmed them, made them smile, much like you.'

'I do?' she exclaimed, astonished and a little embarrassed.

'Mm. People like to be near you, haven't you ever noticed?' And when she shook her head, he continued, 'It's as though you're lucky—no, that's not quite right, it's hard to explain. It's as if whoever you touch, talk to, smile with—oh, I don't know. You make people feel good, charmed.'

'I wish I remembered her,' she began slowly. 'I have only the vaguest memories . . .'

'Excuse me,' a cool, precise voice broke in from behind her, and O'Malley turned, startled, to look into the controlled face of the blonde woman she had seen enter earlier. 'I believe you've just returned from along the coast? That way?' she emphasised, pointing to show which way she meant.

'Yes,' O'Malley admitted cautiously, then watched in some bemusement as the woman delved into her shoulder-bag and produced a photograph which she thrust under her nose.

'Did you see him?'

Staring at the grainy black and white print, her heart lurched alarmingly. Taking it with a hand that trembled slightly, she stared down at the face staring back. The hair was shorter, not exactly neat, but certainly nowhere near as long as it had been when she'd met him. He was clean-shaven too, but the expression was the same, as grim as it had been the last time she saw him. He hadn't wanted his picture taken either, judging by the half-raised arm lifted too late to shield his face. Handing the print back, she shook her head. 'No,' she murmured. 'I haven't seen him.'

With a little dip of her head to Nick, Evelyn

walked away, and O'Malley stared blindly down into her drink.

'That's the first time in your life I've ever known you to lie,' Nick said softly.

Snapping her eyes up to his, she found she couldn't hold his gaze and hastily looked away. 'Who is she?' she queried, one finger rubbing round and round the rim of her glass until the sound put her teeth on edge.

'Newspaper woman,' he murmured absently. 'She's been here all week asking questions, showing that photograph around. O'Malley?' he called softly, and when she looked reluctantly up it was to find his blue eyes full of amused speculation. 'And just where did you meet the infamous Luc Deveraux?'

'Who?' she asked blankly.

'O'Malley?' he said with mock severity. 'The man in the photograph, where did you meet him?'

Her face a study of confusion, she stared at her father for long seconds before saying slowly, 'You know where I met him. I've just finished telling you where I met him.' But all the while she was talking she was turning his name over and over in her mind, savouring it almost. Luc Deveraux. Yes, it suited him exactly.

'O'Malley, if you weren't so big, I'd turn you over my knee and spank you. Where did you meet him?'

'I told you! And what do you mean—*infamous*?' She frowned.

Leaning across the table, his face worried, he said, 'You told me you were kidnapped by Kenneth Dutton, so . . .'

'Kenneth Dutton?' she exclaimed weakly. 'Who the hell is Kenneth Dutton?'

'O'Malley!' he snapped, beginning to lose his temper. 'You told me you were kidnapped by the property developer, Kenneth Dutton, so where did you meet Deveraux?'

Her mouth tight, she articulated clearly, 'I was kidnapped by the man in that photograph, and . . .' She broke off furiously as her father started to laugh. Not a polite chuckle, but a full-bellied roar. She glared impotently at him.

'Oh, darling,' he gasped, 'where on earth did you get the idea that Deveraux was a property developer?'

'Because he told me so, that's why!' she gritted. But had he? she thought. Frowning, she remembered that he hadn't actually said so, not in so many words. Because of his reaction to the knowledge that she was a reporter, she'd assumed he was the property developer. 'Will you stop laughing?' she snapped as Nick's throaty chuckles intruded on her thoughts.

'But it's funny!' he protested, then as he remembered her account of her ordeal, he sobered. 'No, it isn't, is it?'

'No,' she said absently. If he wasn't the property developer, then why had he been so angry at her being connected with the Press? What was he trying to keep secret? 'Pot calling the kettle black,' she'd said. 'Walking all over people.' And he hadn't denied it, had he? So what people had he been treading on? Lifting worried eyes to Nick, she asked, 'If he isn't a property developer, who is he?'

'Luc? He's a photographer.'

'A photographer?' she exclaimed incredulously. 'A photographer? He can't be. He hates photographers!'

'Well, that's what he is,' he said mildly, in direct contrast to her explosion.

'What sort of photographer?' she frowned. 'Press photographer?' Really, the whole thing was getting more ridiculous by the minute. A photographer?

'No. Or not directly. He started out as a war correspondent, then I think he simply got sickened by the butchery, the slaughter, and started taking pictures of the innocent victims instead. The women, children. This was what? Five—ten years ago? At first no one would print them—they were pretty harrowing, it wasn't what people wanted to see, pricked too many consciences, made them think. And then the climate changed and he was suddenly flavour of the month. People couldn't get enough of his pics. He gained a sort of notoriety, a reputation for going where no one else would go: Beirut, Chad, Ethiopia, Sudan. You name it, he went there. He's a bloody-minded so and so, difficult, abrupt, impatient, a one-off, makes his own rules . . .'

'That's him,' she muttered wryly. 'Go on.'

'Well, I don't know much more . . .' He tailed off as he noticed his daughter's expression. 'You liked him, didn't you?' he murmured softly.

'Yes,' she said simply, her cheeks faintly pink, then gave him a rueful little smile. 'But why does he hate the Press so much?' she asked, confused. 'At first, before he found out I was with a photographer . . .'

'He knew you were my daughter?'

'No, just that I was with a photographer. Why? Have you met him?'

'Once, at an award ceremony at the Savoy. He was photographer of the year—he walked out,' he said, grinning as he remembered the furore that had caused. 'He hated all the false back-slapping, the condescension—can't say I blamed him—I'd have walked out, too. Patronising lot!'

'Yes,' she murmured with a faint smile. 'You're a lot alike in some ways.'

'Well, go on,' he said impatiently, 'take that silly smile off your face and tell me the rest! Before he found out, he was what?'

'Nice—no, that's a silly word and certainly doesn't describe him. He was—complete. Humorous in a dry sort of way.' She tailed lamely off. She could hardly tell her father she'd practically begged him to seduce her. Giving a little shrug, she murmured, 'I liked him. Why did the dreaded Evelyn want him? Did she say?'

'No. No, O'Malley, I can't ask her,' he tacked on drily. 'If Deveraux wants to keep his being here a secret from the Press, then I'm not going to be instrumental in getting him found. Come on, let's get some fresh air before she decides to return.'

Smiling, she accompanied him outside. Tucking her hand companionably into his arm, they strolled rather aimlessly down towards the harbour.

'Are you sure he was humorous?' Nick asked with a small, infectious grin. 'Doesn't sound much like the Deveraux I remember.'

'Yes,' she murmured slowly, remembering the little exchanges they had shared. 'Well, maybe not humour, exactly, more like rapport,' she explained, her brow furrowed as she tried to categorise him in her mind. He had seemed to have so many moods that it was difficult to explain the impression she had formed. Feeling her way, she asked hesitantly, 'Nick? Do you know where I might find him?'

'It's important to you?' he asked gently.

'Yes. We were at cross purposes, you see, and although he obviously loathes and despises the Press, of which I am a member, even if only in an obscure way, he hated me because he thought I knew about him—and I didn't. If I don't find him,' she muttered, 'then I'll never know if there could have been more between us.' Really only speaking her thoughts aloud, she asked, 'When you first met Mother, did you know?'

'That she was the one? Oh, yes.' Drawing her to a halt, he searched her face. 'Is it like that, darling?' When she nodded, he squeezed her arm sympathetically. 'And him? Before the misunderstanding? Did he feel the same?'

'I don't know,' she said slowly. 'He liked me—but I don't honestly know if there was anything more. At first I thought so, after we got out of the ruins, but then—oh, I don't know—there seemed a sort of mockery about him, as though he was not only mocking me, but himself.' Turning unhappy eyes on her father, she said softly, 'But I have to try. Do you understand?'

'Yes. I understand. Let's go back to the hotel. I'll

make some calls. Can't promise anything, but I still have one or two contacts.

'Thanks.' Smiling at him, she leaned forward and kissed him warmly on the cheek. As she straightened, she saw Stavros. He was watching them, and one look at his face told her something was very wrong.

Hurrying up to him, a bemused Nick trailing in her wake, she hushed her father with an impatient gesture as he exclaimed angrily on recognising the other man.

'Not now, Nick!' she said shortly. Ignoring his expression of surprise at her rudeness, she turned worriedly back to Stavros. 'What's wrong?' she demanded, then snorted impatiently as Stavros looked pointedly at Nick. 'Never mind him!' she stated bluntly. 'He knows. Go on. Is it Paget?'

'Yes. He's—ill. Infection, I think. He's in the hospital in—in the hospital,' he muttered, clearly not trusting either of them not to divulge his whereabouts to whoever might be interested. Evelyn? she wondered. Did Stavros know about the newspaper woman?

'And you need, what?' she asked impatiently.

'I need someone to stay with Jenny.'

O'Malley didn't ask the obvious question, why couldn't Jenny stay with him? At the moment all that mattered was that they needed help. 'Right,' she said crisply. 'I need a few minutes to pack. Where do I go?'

'I'll be here,' he murmured cautiously.

'Still don't trust me, Stavros?' she asked softly, but without waiting for a reply she dragged her father back to the hotel. 'What the hell is going on, O'Malley?' he demanded. 'And who is Jenny?'

'His daughter,' she explained breathlessly, 'and I have to go with him.'

'I gathered that,' he said drily. 'And what am I supposed to do while you go off on your mission of mercy? Chew my fingernails to the bone? And what infection?' he shouted after her as she dashed into the hotel and took the stairs two at a time.

'I don't have time to explain now. Just stall the dreaded Evelyn if she starts asking questions,' she pleaded, dragging things out of the wardrobe and slinging them into her case. 'To be honest, I don't know what's going on myself, but it obviously has something to do with the newspaper woman. She was the one asking questions and showing his photograph around.' And Paget had been very upset when he'd learned of her connections with the Press. 'Leave my passport, will you? And some money?' As soon as he'd gone, she dragged her dress over her head and pulled on a pair of jeans and a sweatshirt, then stuffed her dress into the case.

When Nick returned from his room, he handed over her passport and a wad of money with a sardonic bow, and she grinned. 'Anything else?' he asked bemusedly.

'Yes. If I don't get back before you leave, I'll see you in London.'

'And that's supposed to comfort me?' he exclaimed.

'I'll be all right,' she said softly, recognising the real worry behind the dry voice. 'Truly.' Giving him a swift hug, she humped her suitcase off the bed and turned to leave.

'Be careful, O'Malley.'

'I will. You know I will. But I have to go, you understand that, don't you?'

'Yes,' he sighed. 'I understand. But if he hurts you, I'll . . .'

'He won't,' she said firmly.

'All right. If you need me, you know where I'll be. Call me.'

'I will. Now, be an angel and make sure the coast is clear, will you? I don't want Evelyn to see me leave.'

Nodding, he preceded her down the stairs, and when he was sure no one was likely to see her departure he hugged her tight before allowing her to race out and down to the harbour.

Stavros was waiting where she'd left him and, taking her case, he led her towards one of the fishing-boats. With one last cautious look round, he helped her on board.

'Down below, O'Malley,' he said shortly.

Nodding, she did as she was told. This was a different Stavros. Authoritative and solely in command. If he said get below, then there was no doubt a damned good reason why she should obey without question. Jenny was hunched up on one of the bunks, her face tearstained, and O'Malley's heart melted. Poor little scrap. She was no doubt as bewildered as herself.

'Hey. What's all this?' she asked kindly. Putting her case on the deck, she dropped down beside her and gathered her into her arms. 'Silly old sausage.'

'Daddy . . .'

'I know, Daddy's not too well, but he's going to be fine, I promise,' she said firmly, crossing her fingers behind Jenny's back. As the engine started up with a low, muted throbbing, she settled herself more comfortably, Jenny cradled in her arms. Peering from the tiny porthole, she watched the quay recede. Well, whatever she had let herself in for, it was too late to retract now, and whatever reasons there were for all this secrecy, they must be important. For the moment, that was sufficient. Besides, she hadn't taken to the newspaper woman one little bit, and thwarting her was as good a reason as any to go along with Stavros. Apart from the very minor fact, of course, that she wanted to see Paget again, she thought with an inward smile. Jenny appeared to have fallen asleep, and she settled her more comfortably against her shoulder before relaxing back against the bulkhead. Brushing the lock of hair back from the little girl's forehead, she stared down at her. So like her father . . . a funny little shiver went through her. Was she being totally stupid? Do you really think he'll take one look at you and decide he can't live without you? No. But he had liked her, she knew he had. Did he even know that Stavros had come to fetch her? She doubted it. Sighing, she closed her eyes. It was barely twenty-four hours since she had seen him, yet it felt like days, so much had happened. She didn't know where they were, or where they were going—and she didn't care. The thought of seeing Paget—Luc, she corrected herself—made her feel alive, excited.

CHAPTER SIX

IT WAS just getting dark when she felt the boat slow and begin to turn, the engine note changing, and she peered through the porthole. She could just make out the large cliff face looming close beside them, rock for the most part, a few sparse clumps of coarse grass clinging stubbornly, and then they were throttling back and the boat bumped gently. The engine was cut and a few seconds later she heard footsteps crossing the deck above her, and she looked towards the companionway, anticipating Stavros's arrival. As his feet, then legs appeared, she gently woke Jenny.

'Ready?' he asked.

'Yes,' she said quietly. As she struggled upright, Jenny still cradled in her arms, Stavros swiftly completed his descent and came to take the little girl from her.

'Can you manage your case?'

'Yes.' Picking it up, she followed him up to the deck. They appeared to be in a kind of natural harbour, a gap or split in the rock face allowed the boat to slip inside—so that it was invisible from the sea? she wondered. A flight of steps led upward, cut into the rock, a wide stone slab at the foot that acted as a landing-stage. Stepping awkwardly from the dipping boat on to the ledge, she stared upward into darkness. There were no lights to illuminate the steps, so with one hand firmly grasping the rail, the other gripping her case, she silently followed Stavros upwards. A villa was perched at the top, a wide flagstoned terrace fronting it. The sea seemed to sigh below them, a low murmur punctuated by the slap of waves against the rock, and she hastened her steps to catch up with Stavros. Skirting the potted shrubs laid out on the flagstones, she joined him at the front door. She could hear the faint hum of a generator, so presumably they would at least have lights, then smiled to herself as Stavros depressed a switch and the wide tiled hall was illuminated with a soft amber glow.

Her first confused glance was of pictures, whitewashed walls, a tapestry in orange and browns, archways. Dropping her case, she followed Stavros through one of them and across a wide expanse of highly polished wood floor with one or two rugs scattered tastefully, then through a door on the far side. Again the room was large, airy, a massive double bed taking pride of place. As Stavros lay Jenny on the soft, multicoloured throwover, O'Malley looked at him. Whoever owned the house had money.

'Paget's?' she asked, and he shook his head, a small, irritating smile on his mouth. Why? What was so amusing about that?

'Does Paget know I'm here?' she asked, and after a short pause he shook his head again, his eyes rueful.

'He isn't going to be very pleased, is he?' she

asked, and wondered why the thought didn't bother her.

'No, O'Malley. He isn't. But there wasn't a choice.'

'Why? Why wasn't there a choice, Stavros?'

Sighing, he murmured, 'Jenny was screaming, hysterical. They wouldn't let her stay at the hospital, and I—er—had things to do, which left only you. Besides, Jenny asked for you, and the only way I could keep her quiet was to promise that I'd fetch you,' he ended lamely. No wiser than she had been before, she gave him a look of wry exasperation.

As though afraid more questions might be forthcoming, he said abruptly, 'I have to go out, I'll be a couple of hours, maybe more. Will you be all right?'

'Yes,' she murmured with another wry smile. Whether she was or she wasn't wouldn't stop him leaving, she knew that very well.

Smiling back, he squeezed her arm. In comfort? Gratitude? 'I'll be as quick as I can,' he murmured. Then, glancing once at Jenny who had gone back to sleep, he added, 'Kitchen's at the end of the passage, help yourself to anything you need.' And then he was gone.

The kitchen was bright, gleaming and efficiently laid out, and O'Malley made herself a cup of coffee and a sandwich before exploring the rest of the villa. Three bedrooms, all with their own bathrooms, a room that was obviously a study. A large, old and battered desk stood in one corner, a typewriter on top. A stack of papers and journals littered the remainder of the surface, and she resisted the temptation to be nosy. There was also a large framed photograph on the shelf above the desk, and she walked across for a closer look. The little girl was definitely Jenny, taken two, or maybe three years before, the woman holding her presumably her mother, Paget's wife. Long, brown hair partially concealed a face that was gentle rather than beautiful, and long, tapered hands seemed to hold the little girl tight, the nails long, unvarnished. Had those nails scored Paget's back? In passion? In need? O'Malley hastily shut that thought off at birth. Being jealous of a dead woman was hardly laudable. Replacing the photograph with an abrupt movement, she turned and went out.

The main living area opened off the room they had walked through earlier, no doorway this time, just another arch. Comfortable-looking leather furniture was scattered rather haphazardly across the wood-block floor, expensive rugs, prints on the walls, but it had an unlived-in look, almost as though whoever owned it had asked a firm of interior decorators to do it, then left it as they had. No personal touches, no plants, the cushions squarely positioned almost to attention. Wide french doors opened out on to another terrace and, curious, she opened the doors and stepped through. The air tasted of salt and she breathed deeply before walking cautiously to the edge of the flagstones. It was difficult to see much in the dark, but she could just make out shrubs, terraced gardens leading down to a kidney-shaped pool. Very nice, very formal, very sterile. Going back inside, she carefully latched the doors behind her and returned to the bedroom.

Kicking off her canvas deck shoes, she lay down beside Jenny, her hands beneath her head, and stared at the ceiling. So many questions and no answers. Why was the newspaper woman looking for him? Why the house that seemed unlived in? Why did Jenny sleep so much? Why, why, why? Her lids slowly closing, she slept.

When she opened her eyes, sunlight was filtering through the window to lie in bars across the end of the bed. It also touched the face of the man watching her and her heart did a crazy somersault. His face held no expression whatsoever, he could almost have been turned to stone, and for long moments she just stared at him blindly, an ache in her throat. His hair was uncombed as though ruffled by sea breezes, his eyes red-rimmed, dark shadows beneath them, and the unshaven jaw was thrust almost pugnaciously as she slowly sat up. He looked dark and dangerous, and very unforgiving.

'You look terrible,' she murmured, her voice husky with nervous excitement.

Without answering, he turned and limped out. Letting her breath out, breath she hadn't been aware she'd been holding, she pulled a *moue* of disgust and disappointment. Careful not to disturb Jenny, she climbed off the bed and padded after him, her bare feet making little squeaking noises on the wood floor. He was standing in the kitchen, his back to her, staring out of the wide window that she saw also overlooked the terrace. His dark drey shirt was pulled tight across his broad, muscled back, and she ached to touch him, hold him. Knowing the sheer futility of doing any such thing, she asked instead, 'How's the leg?'

'Fine,' he said, his voice reflecting total indifference.

Sighing, she turned away to pour herself a cup of coffee from the pot bubbling on the stove. 'I thought you were a property developer,' she said stupidly. 'All our conversations, arguments, were based on that misunderstanding.' Silence. He might have been deaf for all the notice he took. Taking a deep breath, she tried again. 'I don't know what it is you've done, or why Jenny is as she is, it isn't really any of my business . . .'

'No, it isn't,' he interrupted flatly.

'. . . but won't you at least give me the benefit of the doubt?' she continued staunchly. 'Paget!' she stormed in exasperation.

'Don't call me by that ridiculous name!' he said coldly, without turning round.

'All right—Luc, then,' she said impatiently. 'But don't I at least warrant civility after coming all this way to look after Jenny?'

'I didn't ask you to. Nor did I want it.'

'I know you didn't, damn it! Stavros did! But whatever the ins and outs, I'm here, so do you think you could at least have the courtesy to look at me while I'm talking?'

Turning slowly, every movement an insolent statement, he looked at her, and she was even more shocked by his appearance than she had been in the bedroom. There, the dim light had disguised the grey pallor, and her anger was replaced by worry. 'Dear God, Paget, you look terrible. Did the hospital release you?' she asked, unable to believe the medical profession could be so negligent.

'No. I released myself,' said Luc flatly. Then, without change of tone or expression, he added, 'As soon as Stavros gets back, he'll return you to the mainland.'

'Mainland?' she echoed. 'We're on an island?' And, if they were, how had he got back? 'Didn't Stavros bring you here?' she asked in confusion.

'Yes,' he said with cold finality, and pushing past her he walked out and along the hall.

Staring worriedly after him, she slowly finished her coffee, which tasted bitter as gall, then went to shower and change into shorts and top. When would Stavros be back? And where had he gone? Really, she might just as well have stayed with Nick. Luc hadn't been exactly overjoyed to see her, had he? But, even with him hating her as he obviously did, she didn't want to be anywhere else, and she frowned worriedly. How could she have so little pride? She didn't know. All she did know with any certainty was that, even being rude, he made her feel as no other man had ever done. Feminine and soft—and wanton, and she slammed her hand angrily against the tiled wall as tears spurted into her eyes. Damn him! Why did it have to be him?

Jenny was awake when O'Malley came out of the

bathroom, and she forced herself to smile at her. 'Hi, have a good sleep? Why don't you wash and get dressed, and I'll go and get us some breakfast?'

She'd already found that Jenny had a supply of clothes in the oak chest in the corner, and a toothbrush in the bathroom, so they'd obviously been expecting to come here all along. Ruffling the little girl's hair affectionately, she went back to the kitchen.

When they'd eaten, O'Malley washed up while Jenny went to check on her father. She was like a little mother hen with one chick, and when she came back, explaining solemnly that Luc was still asleep, they went to explore outside, Jenny's hand tucked confidently into her own. When Stavros returned from wherever it was he'd been, she and Jenny were sitting on the edge of the pool, dangling their feet in the water. Leaning back on her arms, she squinted up at him. 'Were you with Paget when he discharged himself?' she asked.

'Yes,' he said wryly, 'and if you're about to ask me why I didn't stop him, don't. Trying to stop Luc—Paget——' he corrected comically, and she grinned.

'It's all right, I know his name.'

'Well,' he shrugged, 'when he's set his mind on doing something, it's like trying to stop a tank. It's best to give in.'

'Mm. What did the hospital say?'

'That he was to finish the course of antibiotics, re-dress the leg every day, get plenty of rest and plenty of liquids.'

'Best make sure he does, then, hadn't we?' she murmured, giving him a conspiratorial smile.

'Mm.'

'Except that he said you were to take me back to the mainland as soon as you returned. Only I don't think he ought to be left, do you?' she asked, her eyes innocently wide.

'No. I'm—er—having a bit of trouble with the boat's engine,' he remarked.

'Take a couple of days to get it fixed, do you think?'

'Mm, 'bout that, I reckon.'

Laughing, she called him back as he was about to walk away. 'Stavros? Why did he let me go? Because I thought he was a property developer?'

'Is that what you thought he was?' he asked in astonishment.

'Yes,' she said, staring at him hopefully, but if she expected he might enlighten her she was mistaken. With an odd, thoughtful look in his eyes, he walked away.

'O'Malley?' Jenny asked diffidently.

'Mm?'

'Is it all right now?'

'Yes, darling, of course it is,' she said warmly, giving the little girl a hug. She hadn't the faintest idea whether it was or wasn't, hadn't in fact any idea what they were talking about, but she couldn't question the little girl, for that smacked of unfairness; not that the notion didn't cross her mind, because it did, but she reluctantly decided against it. It was very galling, though. Oh, well, it was another Brownie point to chalk up.

'Are you going to stay now?'

'For a little while,' she said gently. 'A few days.'

For the next two days Luc stayed in his room. She took him drinks, made sure he took his pills and re-dressed his leg, which proved a severe test of her nerves. He always kept the sheet draped modestly across his body, leaving only his injured thigh exposed, but that didn't at all disguise the fact that he was naked beneath it, which made it very difficult to concentrate on the task of changing the bandage. If he noticed her shortened breathing, or that her hands trembled about their task, he didn't mention it, or show by even a look that he had noticed. In fact, he didn't say anything at all, even about her still being there, and naturally O'Malley didn't bring that particular subject up. As withdrawn as he was in her presence, she didn't want to leave. She tried to explain about the mix up over the property developer, discover why he had let her go back to Sophia, but he just shut his eyes, and presumably his ears; certainly, he refused to listen. Frustrated, she'd retreat. Patience was not one of her strongest points, but she was learning. Reluctantly, but she was learning. There wasn't really any other choice. She spent the rest of her time with Jenny, and she was getting rather worried by the dependence the little girl was beginning to show on her. If Luc had his way, she'd be off the island in a few days, and she hated to think that the little girl would be miserable. Conceited, she taunted herself, it's not the little girl that will be miserable, it will be you. Despite their

non-communication, he was there, within touching
distance, so to speak, and all the while she was in his
vicinity, there was a chance to improve relations
between them.

She helped Jenny improve her breast stroke, took
her on rambling walks outside the villa. The island
wasn't large as islands go, about ten miles in length,
she guessed, and they never went out of sight of the
villa, on Luc's strict instructions. She began to
wonder if he was maybe a millionaire, and the threat
of his daughter being kidnapped was what it was all
about. The days slid by with frightening speed, but at
least Jenny seemed to have benefited by her presence.
She no longer looked so weary, although that was
probably natural progression and nothing to do with
her at all. She still took a short nap in the afternoons,
but she was beginning to go brown, and to
O'Malley's untutored eye she looked healthy and fit.
Certainly she seemed to have put on a bit of weight,
because she no longer looked frail, the way she had
before at the house near the ruins. On the fourth
morning, when she went into the kitchen, she saw
Luc was up, and was quite unable to prevent the
surge of excitement she felt. He was dressed in a pair
of shorts and lying on a lounger on the terrace, a cup
of coffee on the flagstones beside him, eyes closed.
He had shaved, and she stared fascinated at the
strong jaw that was a little lighter than the rest of his
face. He looked so different without the growth of
beard—younger, more attractive, if that were
possible. Pouring herself some coffee, she walked out
to join him. He kept his eyes closed, even though he

must have heard her approach.

'How do you feel?'

'Fine.' And she felt like pouring her coffee over his arrogant head. If he said that just once more, she thought she probably would.

'Don't you know any other word?' she exclaimed irritably. When he didn't answer, she leaned back against the doorframe and stared out over the terrace, her jaw thrust out moodily. 'Why did you let me go?' she asked coolly. God, she was beginning to sound like a record stuck in a groove.

Opening his eyes, he stared at her without expression.

'Well?' she demanded crossly.

'Because I no longer wanted you with me,' he said laconically.

'That's no answer!'

'Well, it's all you're going to get,' he said flatly, closing his eyes once more.

'Well, why did you allow me to think you were a property developer, then?' she persisted.

Heaving a sigh that spoke volumes, he sat up and swung his legs over the side of the lounger. 'If you think my gratitude for the care you've given Jenny entitles you to pry into my life, then you're wrong. I want nothing to do with you, O'Malley. End of story.' Getting to his feet, he walked away towards the pool.

Her mouth tight, she emptied the remains of her coffee into the nearest plant-pot, then threw her cup at him. It bounced once on the flagstones, then broke in half. Luc's steps didn't even falter. Gritting her teeth, she stormed after him.

'I didn't ask for your gratitude, neither do I want it! Neither do I have any desire to pry into your life. I'm curious, naturally, and I won't say I wouldn't like to know, because I would, but that's all it is.'

'And you really expect me to swallow that garbage?' he asked incredulously, swinging round to face her. 'You really expect me to believe that all the time we were in Turkey you thought I was a property developer? What was I supposed to develop, for God's sake? The mountains?'

'Don't be stupid!' Then, as her thoughts caught up with his other statement, she frowned. 'We're not in Turkey now?' she asked, puzzled. Well, obviously not, she castigated herself silently, otherwise he wouldn't have said so, would he? They'd been on the boat for how long? Two hours? Three? 'Greece?' she guessed. There were hundreds of islands off Greece.

Giving her a look of disgust, he turned and walked back indoors. 'Luc!' she yelled after him. 'Don't keep walking away when I'm talking to you!' Hurrying after his retreating figure, she followed him into his room. 'My thinking you a property developer was not garbage! Everything you said seemed to fit. You thinking I was with the Press, your reactions. How the hell was I supposed to know you weren't one? I'd never met Kenneth Dutton, I . . .'

'Who?' he asked blankly.

'Dutton! The property developer! I'd never seen a photograph of him, it wasn't until Nick told me who you were . . .'

'Ah! Now we come to it. And that explains a lot as

well. OK, I'll believe you came to Turkey orginally to seek this property developer . . .'

'Magnanimous of you,' she muttered sarcastically. 'And we did not come to seek him out, only find out what he was up to.'

'Whatever,' he said impatiently, ruthlessly interrupting her, 'but when you arrived, something more interesting came along, didn't it, O'Malley? You saw me in the hotel, presumably so too did—Nick . . .'

'You don't need to sneer when you say his name,' she bit out crossly, 'and no, Nick did not see you then.'

'Didn't he?' he asked softly, a rather nasty glint in his eye. 'Didn't he just?'

'No! At least, I don't think so—not then, anyway. He wasn't with me,' she added lamely, because she didn't actually know for sure that Nick hadn't seen him.

'Oh, come on, O'Malley. Do you really expect me to be taken in twice by your fairy-stories? I'm not Stavros. I can't be twisted round your little finger . . .'

'Don't be so damned insulting! To me or Stavros. At least he had the grace to look embarrassed when he lied to me—and why the hell did you tell him to tell me that Sophia had been destroyed? Why allow me to feel all that anguish?'

'Anguish?' he asked incredulously with a short laugh. 'You've never felt anguish in your life! You're selfish and shallow, and you think that because you've always got your own way, you will now! Well, you won't!'

Staring at him in astonishment, at his harsh, angry face, she asked faintly. 'What the hell are you talking about?'

'You, O'Malley!' he bit out, stabbing a finger at her chest. 'You and your pretty ways! Just can't believe you're not irresistible, can you? That some man might not desire you? *Where's your wife*?' he mimicked. *'Dead? Oh, I'm so sorry!* Sorry, hell! You knew all along all there was to know about me. Except this. This one thing. Now there was an interest story, wasn't there? Much more interesting than a blasted property developer!'

'You're insane,' she whispered.

'Oh, you do it well, O'Malley,' he continued in the same flat tone, as though she hadn't spoken. 'I have to give you full marks for that! You really do it well! But I've met hundreds of women like you in my life,' he said scathingly. 'Cheap, selfish, shallow, to whom the end always justifies the means. Women like you, who need constant adulation, change. No one escapes, do they? Any male that comes within your orbit is fair game. Stavros, poor Nick, and if Jenny had been a boy, then no doubt she too would have come in for the charm. Well, not me, O'Malley. I see right through you, right through that beautiful body to the black soul within. I should give up,' he bit out scornfully. 'You're just wasting energy.'

When she didn't answser, for the simple reason that she couldn't think of anything to say, just stared at him, her brown eyes fixed widely, full of hurt, confusion and pain, he gave a thoroughly nasty smile.

'Still want me, O'Malley?' he taunted, as he had taunted in Turkey. Putting out a hand, he tangled a strand of her hair round his finger and tugged, not ungently. 'I'm not averse, you know. You're attractive enough—no, hell, beautiful,' he corrected, his voice deepening, the accent more pronounced, which made O'Malley shiver involuntarily. 'I'd probably even enjoy it.' Sliding his hand round to her jaw, he gripped it, tilting her face towards him. 'Still frustrated, O'Malley?' he asked with cruel mockery. 'Still want to be seduced?'

'No,' she whispered thickly. Then, unable to help herself, she asked miserably, 'Is that really what you think of me?'

'Yes, O'Malley. It's really what I think of you. How many ways do you want it said?' And before she could prevent him, he dragged her fully against him and fastened his mouth on hers in a savage parody of a kiss.

Wrenching her head away, she turned and walked out. There was a hard, tight pain in her chest, a dull ache in her temples. She walked blindly, without thought to her direction. When she was out of sight of his window, she stopped and stared out over the sea. Her breath was jerking painfully in her breast and she pressed her hands hard against her heart to still its thudding. How could she have been so wrong about him? How could she have seen warmth, humour, caring? How could she have thought he liked her? Her hurt went too deep even for tears; there was a tearing, agonising pain inside her and she felt sick. But there were no tears. She didn't know

how long she stood there, probably only minutes, yet
it seemed a lifetime before she turned and went to her
room. Packing quickly, she carried her case to the
top of the steps, her mind determinedly blank, her
eyes painfully dry. Seeing the boat moored below,
Stavros on deck, she slowly descended.

'Will you take me to the mainland?' she asked
quietly, her voice croaky and uneven.

Staring at her, taking in the wide, unhappy eyes,
the still face, he nodded. 'Here, give me your case,'
he said gruffly. Helping her on board, he quickly
untied the mooring-rope, then hastened to the engine
and kicked it into life. As he steered them out into the
open sea, O'Malley perched on the little seat beside
him and kept her face resolutely forward.

'I'm sorry, O'Malley,' he said quietly.

'It doesn't matter,' she replied listlessly. She
doubted Stavros even knew what he was apologising
for, but that didn't matter either. 'It's my own fault.
I saw something in him that just wasn't there.'

She thought for a moment he was going to tell her,
explain, only he didn't, just gave a long sigh. 'Shall I
take you back to Sophia?' he asked gently.

'No. The nearest mainland will do.' She didn't feel
like facing her father and the sympathy she knew she
would see in his face.

He dropped her just outside Lavrion; she'd be able
to get a bus from there into Athens, he told her.
Nodding, thanking him quietly, she said goodbye.
'Give my love to Jenny,' she whispered. Taking her
case, she trudged away. She thought she felt about a
hundred years old.

She found a cheap hotel in a side street and rang her father from there; she'd see him when she saw him, in London. He didn't try to persuade her to come home straight away, merely cautioned her to be careful. She also put a call into the magazine, only to be told, not unexpectedly, that she no longer had a job. The magazine had folded. Well, all ties temporarily severed. She'd bum around Europe, she suddenly decided. See and do all the things she'd never had time for. Except that she didn't feel like doing any of them.

CHAPTER SEVEN

O'MALLEY caught a flight from Athens to Rome, using her credit card; she'd worry about her finances when she got home. She then spent six weeks making her way up through Italy, Genoa, Monaco and into France. She took odd jobs where she could to spin out her money, waitressing, planting crops, hard, backbreaking work that sublimated thought. Those first few weeks, the only way she could cope was to blank things out, not think about him. By the time she reached Calais, she thought she had come to terms with her hurt. What she could not come to terms with were his words. Each one was imprinted indelibly on her brain. Cheap, selfish, shallow, a woman who needed constant adulation, and she couldn't rid herself of the thought that they were partially true. Hadn't she almost come to the same conclusions herself in Turkey? She *was* selfish, and then forced herself to dredge her mind for instances that would prove it. Didn't she always do what she wanted to do? She conveniently forgot that there were others, apart from Nick, that she had to consider. Shallow, too. Didn't she live life on the surface? Lots of people had told her that, told her she was lucky she didn't feel things too deeply. But she did, she just never allowed them to show. Nick had taught her that—never give in

to pain, hide sorrow from others, other people don't
want to be burdened with your troubles, they
probably have enough of their own.

And as for needing constant adulation—well, she
enjoyed it, didn't she? Liked to be whistled at,
enjoyed being told she was beautiful—God, she was
probably conceited as well. Had he forgotten that
word? He must have done, or he'd have hurled that at
her as well. She chopped and changed jobs, was
impulsive, thoughtless. In fact, the more she thought
about herself, the more depressed she became. And
how arrogant to assume that he would like her! That
Jenny would miss her. That Stavros had felt
compassionate. All he'd probably felt was
embarrassment. By the time the ferry docked in
Dover, she felt as though a very dear friend had died.

She caught a train to Waterloo, then a tube to
Hampstead, and the cheerful greeting of the ticket
collector only added to her misery. Cheer up, he said.
How could she cheer up? Giving him a lame smile, she
trudged to the bus stop. If her father wasn't in, then
she'd go to her flat near Blackfriars. But she needed to
see Nick first, let him know she was all right, and she
gave a dreary little laugh. Nick would probably think
she'd run mad. Normally after she hadn't seen him for
a while, she just rang when she got round to it. So
selfish. Well, she could change, couldn't she?

Ellen Dove, Nick's housekeeper, answered the door
to her ring, and with a warm smile, showed her into
her father's study. He was sitting in the worn old
leather chair that he refused to replace. The dim light
silvered his gold hair, and the saggy cardigan he was

wearing gave the illusion of an elderly gentleman wrapped against the cold. He had never looked more dear.

'Hello, Nick,' she said softly.

The surprise on his face told her that he hadn't heard her enter, and then he was leaping to his feet and hastening across the room to give her a bearhug that nearly broke her ribs, but went a long way to comforting her.

'O'Malley!' he exclaimed. Then, forcing her away from him, retaining a grip on her arms, he gave her tanned face a thorough scrutiny. 'My dear girl, you look terrible. Are you all right?'

'Yes. A bit battered and bruised, and if not altogether bowed, then pretty close . . .' She was as horrified as he when her voice broke.

'Oh, good heavens!' he exclaimed softly. 'Come on, come and sit down. Tell your old man all about it. A trouble shared is a trouble halved.'

O'Malley looked at him in astonishment. 'I thought it was, "Don't tell me your troubles, I have troubles of my own"'!

'Is it?' he asked, looking for all the world as if she'd just told him she'd seen a tiger on the heath. 'Well, perhaps it is. Anyway, come and sit down, I expect Ellen will bring some tea.' And she gave a grunt of amusement.

'Oh, Daddy,' she murmured helplessly, because Ellen always brought tea.

'You haven't called me that since you were a little girl,' he said softly. 'Is it so bad, O'Malley?'

'Yes. No. Oh, I don't know. I'm just tired, I guess.'

Collapsing down on to the sofa, she pushed the heavy weight of hair off her face.

When Ellen had brought in the tray, Nick took her hand in his. As he gave her nails a minute examination, she stared at him curiously, then wondered with some trepidation what was coming. Nick behaving awkwardly was decidedly unusual, and, with her own troubled thoughts about herself still fresh in her mind, she felt somewhat alarmed.

'He was here,' he said quietly, moving his eyes to hers. It was the last thing she expected to hear, and her eyes widened in shock. 'A month ago.' She had no need to ask who, why was a different matter. 'He didn't say much, not about why he wanted to see you, anyway. Tore me off a strip for letting you wander round Europe unaccompanied, seemed to think I should have been worried or something.' And they exchanged a long, smiling look, because of course he had been worried about her, she knew that, as she would have been about him, but it seemed extraordinary all the same. Why would Luc do something so odd? It didn't make any sort of sense. 'What happened?' he asked softly.

'Nothing much,' she murmured on a long sigh. 'Bit arrogant of me, wasn't it? To assume he'd feel the same.' Finding her voice wouldn't work properly, but persisted in breaking in the middle of each sentence, she got to her feet and went to stand at the window. It might be easier to explain if she kept her back to her father. Didn't have to see his face. 'Turned out he didn't even like me. Apparently I'm amoral, selfish, conceited, probably a nymphomaniac to boot. He's met women like me before, it seems. Ah, well,' she said sadly, trying to sound philosophical, when all she wanted to do was weep. 'A lesson learned.'

'Then why did he come?' Nick asked gently.

'Probably thinks I took something—papers, family silver, who knows?' To think anything else would be stupid and only lay herself open to more heartache. Anyway, she hated him, didn't she?

'I didn't somehow get the feeling he was after stolen silver,' Nick remarked drily. He wanted very much to hold her, comfort her, take away the pain. There was something she wasn't saying, and he dearly wanted to know what it was. He knew she was hurting badly, and he wondered how best to go about getting her to explain properly instead of skating over the incidents. Much like he did himself, he thought ruefully. The deeper the hurt, the more light-hearted the tone. It fooled most people, but not him. 'He asked me to let him know when you came back,' he added casually.

'But you won't, will you,' she said, not asking, not in query, but as a statement of fact.

'No. Not if that's what you want . . . What will you do now?'

'Oh, look for a job. Finances are definitely a bit shaky. The job at the magazine folded, did I tell you?'

'Mm,' he murmured absently. 'Stay here for a bit, keep your old man company. Ellen has kept an eye on your flat, given it a clean, an airing, picked up any post. You've no reason to rush away, have you?'

'No.' And, in truth, the idea appealed. Nick was good company, and might help to keep her brooding thoughts at bay. 'OK, thanks, I'll stay a few days

anyway, get my act together, as they say. I'll go and
see Ellen about getting my room ready.' Although she
found it very hard to interest herself in anything. She
felt dead, empty.

Later that evening, as they sat opposite each other in
the old, squashy armchairs, her thoughts reverted to
those that had been her constant companion since
she'd left the island. Then, with what she fervently
hoped was a casual air, she asked, 'Would you say I
was very arrogant?'

'No,' he replied, keeping his attention very firmly
fixed on his book, not one word of which he was
taking in.

'Selfish, then?'

'No. Anybody less selfish would be hard to find,'
he said mildly.

Heaving a big sigh of exasperation, she muttered,
'Well, shallow? Would you say I was shallow?'

'No, O'Malley, I wouldn't,' he said firmly,
lowering his book. 'I would say you are lovely, warm-
hearted, positive, courageous.'

'But seeking constant adulation?' she persisted.
Good heavens, there must be some fault her father
could see? Surely he wasn't that blind?

'O'Malley, a man will say a lot of things when he's
in a temper. He will dig up the nastiest taunts he can
find—usually because they are the exact opposite of
what he is feeling! You said he liked you! Well, there
you are, then. He suddenly discovers, or thinks he
discovers, that you have feet of clay—and if you've
been worrying yourself sick, psychoanalysing yourself,

believing even one taunt, then I'm ashamed of you. If you have a fault, it's that you're too impulsive, that you let your heart rule your head! If anyone else had hurled those sort of insults at you, someone you weren't emotionally involved with, you'd have hurled back some of your own! Wouldn't you? And never for one moment would you have believed them to have any truth. My guess is that he's discovered he was wrong about you and has come to apologise.' Giving her one long look, he returned his attention to his book.

Extending her legs, she stared thoughtfully at her feet as she mulled over his words. Maybe he was half-right, she conceded. Maybe her unhappiness and hurt had blown it up out of all proportion. 'But I do chop and change my jobs pretty often. That's sort of shallow, isn't it?'

'O'Malley! Any fault, or any virtue come to that, depends on whose yardstick you use. Doesn't it?'

'Yes,' she admitted cautiously.

'Well, then! Just because you need—no, *like*, a challenge, doesn't mean you're shallow, it just means you have itchy feet! And if Luc believes all the things he said about you, then that's his problem. It doesn't mean you have to change to fit the mould of the person he thinks you should be—because if you do, then you'd be living a lie. To thine own self be true, O'Malley. It's a good maxim.'

'Yes,' she agreed. Heaving a big sigh, she got to her feet and went across to drop a light kiss on her father's hair. 'Love you,' she murmured. 'I think I'll go to bed. Night.'

'Night, darling.' Watching his daughter walk from the room, he slammed his book shut. If Luc came back, he thought he'd very likely punch him on the jaw. Damned fool!

O'Malley lay awake for a long time, thinking over Nick's words, but came to no great conclusion. There was no escaping the fact that Luc had said them, which meant he must have thought them. It would be best just to put him out of her mind. Anyway, she could never forgive him for the things he'd said. But why had he come to see her? She hoped it wasn't anything to do with Jenny, then was irritated with herself for even speculating. Hadn't she just told herself to put him out of her mind? Only she couldn't. She wanted him, dammit! She wanted him to want her! Turning her face into the pillow, she cried quietly, very conscious of the fact that her father slept in the room on one side of her, Ellen on the other. But oh, it hurt so, this wanting, this ache inside. What was it that made him so different from all the other men she had met? Why should green eyes and a harsh face haunt her?

She registered at all the local employment agencies, went for long solitary walks on the heath, but he was still there, always there in her thoughts. The warmth, the humour, the mockery, like an unwelcome ghost. She should hate him, tried desperately to do so, despise him, forget him, only she couldn't, she could only analyse her own behaviour, try to see where she had gone wrong. Returning home two days later from yet another walk, her beautiful thick hair beaded with moisture from the fine drizzle, she hung her mac on the hall peg and wandered through into the lounge.

Luc was standing at the window, his back to the room, and she halted in shock, her heart somersaulting. His hands were linked behind his back as he gazed out into the garden, and she stared at him greedily. His hair was still too long, overlapping the collar of his white shirt, and instead of the jeans she was used to he wore a pair of grey trousers that looked as though they'd been pressed to within an inch of their life. They moulded his strong thighs and emphasised the length of his legs. Moving her eyes reluctantly away from him, she stared helplessly at Nick. He was sitting in the armchair, Jenny on his knee, a book open between them. Only Jenny spoke.

'Hi, O'Malley,' she said brightly, giving a gap-toothed grin as though everything was normal, that her visit to them was an everyday occurrence. 'I lost my tooth. Look?'

Smiling faintly, O'Malley murmured softly. 'So I see.' She was aware that Luc stiffened at her words, but he didn't turn round. Nick just eyed her sardonically over the little girl's head.

'Nick and me is reading,' Jenny continued happily, obviously quite impervious to the strained atmosphere, and she held up the book so that O'Malley could see. 'It's good.'

'Yes,' she said lamely, her voice a husky thread of sound. 'Dr Seuss.' The book was *The Cat in the Hat Came Back*, and she wanted to laugh hysterically—it seemed so terribly appropriate. She wondered if that was Nick's idea of a joke. Fortunately, before the whole thing could degenerate into pure farce, Ellen came in bearing a tea tray, and she thought she had never been more grateful for an interruption in her life.

'Thanks, Ellen,' said Nick, sounding for all the world as though he was about to burst out laughing, and O'Malley glared at him.

Walking across to the armchair, she collapsed into it as though her legs would no longer support her, and busied herself pouring the tea. 'Would you like a drink, Jenny?'

'Please,' she said carefully, glancing at her father as she did so, a rather proud look on her face, and O'Malley guessed it was because she was being treated as a grown up, being offered tea in a cup like anyone else.

'Nick?'

'Mm.'

'Luc?' she managed, forcing the word past her dry throat. He turned then, his beautiful eyes subjecting her to a thorough scrutiny, and she looked hastily away. She'd never been a coward in her life, but wanted to be one now. Wanted to rush away, hide in her room. She was aware of every step he took, every muscle movement as he came across to take his tea from her. The very air seemed charged with a terrible tension which didn't lessen in the least as he retreated a few paces away from her and moved his eyes to his cup. His brows were drawn into a frown, and the familiar lock of hair fell across his forehead, and she sighed. Her feelings hadn't changed at all; intensified, if anything. She still wanted him, unbearably. But what did he want?

'Oh, this is ridiculous,' she muttered, plonking her cup down on the coffee-table. Her nerves wouldn't take much more, she just wanted to get it over with.

'Why don't you take Luc into the study, darling? You'll be able to talk there, and Jenny and I can get back to our story.'

Scowling at him, a threat in her lovely eyes that she would talk to him later, she got to her feet and turned to stare at Luc. 'Well?' she demanded.

Exchanging a glance with her father, which infuriated her, and carefully placing his cup on the window-ledge behind him, Luc glanced back at her, his face carefully blank.

Whirling round, she walked out, her movements still and awkward. Pushing into the study, she went to stand at the window, her hands gripped together in front of her. She heard the study door close and she waited, her heart fluttering madly in her chest, her mind a seething mass of unconnected thoughts.

'How are you, O'Malley?' he asked, and his voice too sounded rusty, unused.

'Fine,' she answered flatly, and she heard him sigh. If she didn't look at him, look into those impossibly beautiful eyes, perhaps it would be all right. She felt so lacking in confidence, it was ludicrous—only, all those things he had said still filled her mind, and it was almost as if it were yesterday that he had said them. 'I don't want you here!' she said fiercely.

'No,' he agreed.

'Then why?' she burst out. 'Why did you come?

Was it Nick who told you I was back?'

'No.'

'Then how did you know?' Because he had known, she knew he had, knew he hadn't come on the off-chance.

'I've had someone watching the house,' he said simply, and she gave a dreary little laugh.

'Figures. Still think I'm trying to smear your name?' she asked bitterly. 'Well, I'm not! I don't give a damn what you're up to.' Swallowing quickly as her voice wobbled uncertainly, she husked, 'How's Stavros?'

'Fine.' And that one word, that one word that he always used, that she too seemed to have adopted, sent such a rush of anger and bitterness through her, that she turned to confront him, her eyes hard and bright in her still face.

'Then why are you here?'

'To apologise, explain.'

'Apologise?' she asked incredulously. 'It's a bit late for that, isn't it?' Weeks too late, she thought as she remembered all the heart-searching, the misery. 'You hurt me!' she shouted.

'I know. I came after you to apologise, but you'd already gone and there was no way I could follow you until Stavros returned. He took me back to the mainland, but I couldn't find you.' His eyes were empty, she saw—dull—and she searched his face for the truth of his statement. 'Jenny was crying,' he continued in the same quiet voice. 'Stavros giving me a hard time, not that he said anything I didn't already know. I was angry, O'Malley,' he murmured, as though that explained everything, 'and then when I got back, that damned Tyson woman was there.' Giving a humourless laugh, he added, 'Tall, blonde and hard as bloody nails—and I wanted to hit her.' Taking a deep breath, he pushed his hands into his trouser pockets and, rocking backwards and forward on the balls of his feet as though being forced to stand still and explain was testing him to the limit, he continued flatly, 'I slung her off the island and Stavros took me to Sophia, to the hotel. Nick had already left. I got his full name and address from the register. Why in God's name didn't you tell me you were his daughter?' he exclaimed. 'None of the misunderstandings would have happened if you'd told me that! And to go tramping half-way round Europe——' he gritted scathingly. 'How could you do anything so criminally stupid?'

'Stupid?' she echoed, staring at him incredulously. 'Did you expect me to shrug off your insults? Dismiss them? I was hurt, dammit!'

'I know,' he admitted wearily. 'I'm sorry.'

'Sorry?' she repeated. 'And that makes it right? Cancels it all out?' Giving a defeated little sigh, and hating herself for the need to know, she looked down, then asked quietly, 'Did you mean them? Those things you said?'

'Oh, O'Malley! Of course I didn't mean them. I was angry, hurt, lashing out . . .'

'But you must have thought them, or you wouldn't have said them, would you?' she persisted. Looking up, only to find he was staring at her as though he'd never seen her before in his life, she hastily turned her back and resumed her contemplation of the damp garden.

'I thought them true of the woman I thought you were,' he said carefully. 'The sort of woman Evelyn Tyson is.'

'I'm nothing like Evelyn Tyson,' she muttered crossly.

'No. But I thought you were. When we were at the house in Turkey, and Stavros went to find out the extent of the earthquake . . .'

'The supposed extent of the earthquake!' she gritted, swinging round to face him again. 'Why? Why did he tell me Sophia was destroyed?'

'Because when he went there and discovered that a tall, blonde newspaper woman had been asking questions,' he retorted, clearly irritated at being diverted from his set speech, 'a woman moreover who was accompanied by a photographer, he assumed, as I did when he told me, that you were she. If Sophia was destroyed, then there would be no telephone lines, so if you were unable to file your story quickly, you were less likely to make a very determined effort to escape. Also, being a newspaper women, you would know that the only stories to be given priority would be those dealing with the earthquake.'

'Only of course I didn't assume any of that,' she muttered sarcastically, 'because I had no story to file.'

'No.'

'Then why not just bloody well ask me?' she demanded bitterly.

'Because it never occurred to me that you weren't she!' he said impatiently. 'If you'd told me Nick was

your father, explained about your name—how the hell
was I supposed to know that you really were called
O'Malley? That Nick was your father? I thought he
was your damned lover!'

'Yes, just another conclusion you jumped to,' she
muttered. And how come it was suddenly all her
fault?

'Well, what else was I supposed to think? I'm not
phychic, for God's sake! Why couldn't you just
explain?'

'Because I thought you were the property
developer, didn't I?' she exclaimed furiously. 'And
when I tried at the island villa, you wouldn't blasted
well listen! And anyway,' she went on as she
remembered something else, 'you were all right at
first, so if you thought I was lying about my name,
why not say so then?'

When he didn't answer, she turned to peer at him
and her eyes widened as she registered his air of
embarrassment. 'Well?'

'I thought you were playing games,' he murmured
wryly.

'Games?' she queried, bewildered. 'What sort of
games?'

'Sexual games.'

'Sexual . . . Oh, I see,' she exclaimed as enlighten-
ment dawned. 'Girl meets boy, coyly plays games to
promote interest . . .' She saw by his face that she was
right. 'Oh, for goodness' sake! I'm twenty-eight, not
eighteen!'

'You think that makes a difference?' he asked

cyncially. 'In my experience it doesn't matter if they're five or fifty!'

In my experience, she repeated silently. Yes, she supposed he would have had a lot of experience, none of it very good, judging by his expression. 'Well, you weren't damned well averse!' she muttered, averting her eyes again. Suddenly feeling incredibly tired, she pushed the heavy weight of hair off her neck. Staring blindly at the rain-drenched hollyhocks outside the window, she continued, 'Anyway, what does it matter now? It's all immaterial.'

'No, it isn't! How the hell do you think I felt when I discovered I was wrong!'

'I don't know, do I?' she snapped irritably. Picking absently at a loose flake of paint on the windowsill, she asked quietly, 'Why was Evelyn looking for you?' When he didn't answer, she turned to stare at him. His face held a curious blankness, his eyes steady on hers, and she burst out bitterly, 'Oh, I see, still not to be trusted, am I?'

'It's not a question of trust. I . . .'

'Isn't it? Or are you now about to accuse me of telling her where you were?'

'No.' Staring at her, his eyes brightly green in that carved, still face, he suddenly sighed and ran a hand wearily through his hair. It was shorter, but hardly tidier; it looked as though he'd hacked it about himself. He also looked very tired, and she wondered if his leg was still troubling him. Only she wasn't going to ask. She knew the answer she would get. Fine. 'She tracked me down through Stavros . . .'

'You aren't going to tell me Stavros told her,

because that I won't believe.'

'No. And will you please let me finish a sentence?' he rasped irritably.

'Oh, well, that was more like it, the Luc we all know and love!' she sneered. 'I was wondering how long the humility would last.' And why on earth was she being so damned awkward and disagreeable? She wanted his explanations, didn't she? Answers to all those puzzles? Yes, but she was also terrified he would guess how she still felt about him, and she couldn't, *wouldn't* lay herself open to any more scathing comments. She knew she wouldn't be able to take them again. Her wounds had only a very fragile skin over them. And he'd only said he'd come to apologise and explain. He'd never said he'd wanted more, even before their misunderstandings. She could hardly suppose that had changed. It had been she who'd done all the running. She couldn't forget that.

'O'Malley,' he gritted, 'I am not the most patient of men. I find explanations tedious, to say the least, but I need and want you to understand, and then perhaps we can stop playing with words and both say what we need to!'

'I don't need to say anything!' she stormed, refusing to analyse what that might mean. 'I . . . Let me go, Paget!' she yelped, startled as he strode across the room and grabbed her arms above the elbows.

'Luc!' he put in softly, his face thrust close to hers. 'And heaven help me, O'Malley, if you don't keep still and just listen I'll . . .'

'What? Strangle me?' she taunted, her voice sounding as though he was doing just that.

'No—kiss you,' he breathed huskily, his eyes suddenly darkening. Her heart lurched unevenly.

'No,' she protested hoarsely, unable to drag her own eyes away from the bright intent of his. 'You do, and I'll—I'll scream!' Oh, very heroic, O'Malley, she castigated herself. Very feminist. And why would he want to kiss her, anyway? Because it was the most effective way of shutting her up?

As he dragged a deep breath into his lungs and held it there for a moment, his eyes briefly closing, she couldn't make up her mind if it was in exasperation with her, or himself, or just to contain his temper. Certainly his jaw was clenched, and then he released her and took a step away, as though he couldn't trust himself not to—what? Kiss her or strangle her? she wondered as she continued to stare at him almost blindly. 'No,' he murmured almost to himself. 'No, that won't solve anything. Just listen, please.'

And she just bet that was a first for him as well, saying please. And kissing her *would* solve something, she thought sadly. Just his touch had proved that. But she didn't honestly think he had come to tell her he'd fallen wildly in love with her.

'You have ten minutes,' she managed, sounding grudging even to herself as she fought to keep her emotions under control, because his nearness, his voice that slid like liquid treacle down her spine, were undermining all her hardfound resolutions. But pride at least dictated that she try and keep her end up, not stand there like some dummy. She'd been duped by him once before, she wasn't about to let him do so again. A sexy voice and green eyes altered nothing. At least, they didn't if he didn't want her.

'Evelyn Tyson tracked me down through Stavros,' he resumed slowly. 'When she couldn't find me, she began checking through the records of old friends of mine, of whom Stavros is one. It was no secret that he owned a villa on an island off Greece . . .'

'Stavros owned it?' she asked in astonishment, her interest captured again. So that was why he'd smiled. 'Good grief, he'd looked as though he didn't even own a decent pair of shoes!'

'No.' Then, giving a little grin that crumbled her resolutions all over again, he added, 'Stavros is a millionaire several times over.' He laughed openly at her look of incredulity. 'He owns property all over the place. If anyone was a property developer, it was him.' Which was quite the wrong thing to say, because it reminded O'Malley of the anguish and heartache this man had put her through. Something he must have seen for himself, because his smile died and he sighed again.

'And why would a millionaire several times over dress like a pirate?' she asked haughtily.

'Because he's a friend. Because he knows I would do the same for him—anyway, he was enjoying himself hugely.' With a small, reminiscent smile that irritated her, he murmured, 'He'd just finished an endurance course to keep himself fit, and he wanted to put it into practice. Only I think he got a little more than he bargained for,' he said softly as his eyes held hers, and O'Malley knew he was referring to her mountain climbing that had gone so disastrously wrong.

'He was nice,' she mumbled lamely.

'Yes. He liked you too—it hurt him to have to lie to you.'

'But not you,' she couldn't resist pointing out.

'You think it didn't hurt me?' he asked flatly, his eyes hard. Only O'Malley wasn't even going to attempt to answer leading questions, and she turned her shoulder.

Taking a deep breath that sounded extremely weary, he continued, 'Anyway, that was how she found us.'

'Because?' she put in stiffly.

'Because I had just kidnapped Jenny,' he said without expression, and if he had hoped to astonish her further he succeeded, because she just stared at him in stupefaction. Out of all the things she had thought of, puzzled out, kidnapping his daughter was not among them.

'Kidnapped?' she asked weakly.

'Yes.'

'But why? Why did you need to kidnap your own daughter? She *is* your daughter?' she asked warily.

'Yes.' Rubbing a tired hand over his face and round to the back of his neck, as though it were aching, or tense, he muttered, 'It's—complicated.'

When she made a sound of impatience, he began slowly. 'Two years ago, I was on an assignment in South Africa, and what with one thing and another, I was there nearly six months. No news could get in or out. Not that they even bloody tried!' he burst out in remembered anger. 'When I eventually got home it was to find that my wife had died a month after I'd left and that her parents had custody of Jenny. I didn't even learn it from them, but from a neighbour! Peritonitus. Peritonitus, in this day and age, all because she was afraid to make a fuss,' he said bitterly. 'Her parents assumed, or wished, that I was dead or imprisoned, so they took Jenny to live with them—in Spain. Not that I knew that at the time.'

'But surely the law was on your side . . .' she began, puzzled.

'Of course it was!' he bit out irritably. 'But the law takes time, especially if they can't find the people concerned. They'd already had her five months before I found out—and if they thought I was going to leave my daughter in their hands indefinitely to be brainwashed the way Anita had been . . .' Breaking off, his face working, he stared blindly at the wall, his hands bunched into fists.

'Go on,' she prompted softly, her lovely eyes full of compassion.

Taking a deep, steadying breath, he resumed, 'For you to understand, I have to go back to the beginning.' And, when she nodded encouragingly, he murmured, 'Anita was an only child, her parents quite elderly when they had her. They did her thinking for her, dictated how her life should be, what she should do, shouldn't do. Needless to say, what she shouldn't have done was marry me!' he snapped bitterly. Then he added more quietly, 'Neither should I have married her, that was one of my more spectacular mistakes!'

'Why?' she put in softly, needing to know.

Moving away from her, his body projected the utter weariness he was feeling, he leaned one shoulder against the wall and she stared much as she had done through the window. Maybe he too found it easier to speak when he wasn't facing her. 'It seemed as though I'd been involved in fighting and bloodshed all my life. I was sick and tired, gorged on suffering. When I came back from the Middle East, I took my films into the photographic studio I used, and there was Anita. She was like a breath of fresh air, a calm oasis after a storm, and like a fool, without waiting to find out more about her, get to know her properly, I married her. I thought she was what I needed to give my life purpose, the total antithesis of all I'd ever known. She was gentle and sweet, not a malicious bone in her body —and I knew before the month was out that I'd made a dreadful mistake. Her gentleness and constant understanding began to drive me insane—and that made me feel guilty. I didn't very much like the feeling.' Taking a deep breath, he said flatly, 'I'm the first to admit that I'm arrogant, impatient, whatever, but there is nothing more guaranteed to drive me into a greater fury than someone agreeing with every damned word I say.' O'Malley hastily repressed the involuntary twitch of her lips. She couldn't think of anything more infuriating herself.

'Not only that, I discovered that my lovemaking shocked her, nakedness was sinful, bodies should be covered at all times. I couldn't believe that in this day and age anyone could be so innocent. Then I discovered that her mother had instilled into her from birth that men were filthy, disgusting creatures who only wanted one thing, and it was a woman's duty to deny them. God only knew why her father stayed

married to her mother!' Giving a harsh laugh, he
turned a twisted face towards her, and O'Malley wanted so very much to go to him, but the expression in his
eyes warned her off. He did not want her pity, nor her
understanding, it seemed, just wanted her to listen.

'It was one hell of a mess. When I offered her a
divorce, she became hysterical. Her parents had been
against the marriage from the start, how could she
confess to them that she had been a failure? So we
decided to stay together, but the marriage would be
platonic, and after that she seemed quite contented. I
think, in truth, I terrified the life out of her. God
knows why she agreed to marry me in the first place,
or maybe all she really wanted was to have a house of
her own, get away from her family. I don't know.
Knowing Anita, I don't even suppose she thought
about the physical side to marriage. She was inclined
to live in cloud cuckoo land, and she probably just
shut her mind to it like she did everything else. Yet
maybe if it had been anyone else but me, she would
have coped. Maybe I wasn't as gentle with her as I
could have been, though heaven knows I tried.'

No, he wouldn't have been gentle, not in a hesitant
sense, anyway, she thought. He would have been
eager and demanding, passionate, needing a woman
with an appetite as great as his, and she shivered,
regret and longing filling her. She would have
answered all his needs and gladly. Only he hadn't
wanted her to, and she supposed that after his gentle
Anita she would appear wanton, conceited. Hastily
she dragged her attention back to find he was still
talking and she wondered how much she had missed.

'. . . unfortunately, by that time she was pregnant, another complication. I gave up foreign assignments to be with her because I knew damned well she'd never cope with that on her own. I felt stifled, and then guilty for feeling that way. No one had forced me, it was my own fault, all of it. We plodded along, neither happy nor unhappy, and as soon as I thought she could cope with Jenny, when she was about three, I began accepting foreign assignments—until the last one, in South Africa.' Lapsing into silence, he stared blindly into the garden for a long moment, and O'Malley guessed he was reliving that time.

'Anyway,' he continued eventually, 'the first thing I did when I found out was to go round to her family to see what the hell was going on. They'd moved. No one knew where they'd gone. It took me eighteen months to track them down.' And his words were bitten out, painfully, as though even now he could not bear to remember that awful time. It must have been awful, and she tried to imagine him tramping round town after town, country after country, searching for his daughter.

'Oh, Paget, I'm so sorry.' Moving towards him, she lay a gentle hand on his arm which he either didn't see, or chose to ignore, and she let it fall limply to her side.

'No, I could not have my daughter, they said. I was an unfit father, I did not deserve to have custody of a delicate little girl! I was never there, I drank too much, swore, kept bad company. All of which was probably true, but she was my child! Mine! Not theirs! I loved her, O'Malley,' he said fiercely, suddenly focusing on her face, 'despite the farce of my marriage, and no damned sanctimonious do-gooders were going to take her away from me! They'd ruined their own daughter, and they sure as hell weren't going to ruin mine! So I bided my time. My first attempt to take her was thwarted because she contracted glandular fever and I had to wait until she was better . . .'

'That was why she was always tired,' she mused.

'Yes. Her illness gave me time to make arrangements: the villa in Greece that belonged to Stavros, my own lawyers in France to sort out the legalities in case they tried to make her a ward of court, although living in Spain made it easier for me. They had no legal standing in that country as they weren't nationals. But I wasn't going to take the chance of them trying to snatch her back! She was mine, O'Malley, and I was going to damned well keep her!'

'I see. And not me, nor anyone else was going to ruin it,' she said softly, her voice resigned.

'No,' he said quietly, his eyes searching hers, but she wasn't sure for what. Understanding? Approbation? 'I couldn't take the chance of it getting out, of my whereabouts being known until I got confirmation that Anita's parents would leave well alone. Neither did I want our names plastered all over the newspapers. Jenny was still wary, bewildered. She hardly remembered me,' he said with soft bitterness. 'And for all I knew you could have been working for them.'

'Yes.' What else could she say? She understood why he'd behaved as he had, but, thinking that, had he needed to say all those things? Why not just remain remote? Silent? 'So what were you doing in Turkey?'

'The damned boat broke down. We put into Sophia. That day you saw me in the hotel, I was ringing my lawyers to explain that I would be out of contact for a while. Stavros was making arrangements for somewhere for us to stay—the house where I took you belonged to some friends of his. He bought an old truck, provisioned the house . . .'

'And that day at the ruins? You were waiting for the boat?'

'What? Oh, yes. As soon as it was fixed, a fisherman friend of Stavros was to pick us up. We arranged for it to be at dusk—only of course we didn't know which day. So each day at the appointed time one of us would go to look.'

'I see. So that was where Stavros kept disappearing to?' And when he nodded, she continued, 'And it's all sorted out now?'

'Yes.'

'Yes,' she echoed. 'Well,' she added on a deep breath, 'thank you for explaining, I hope all goes well for you.'

'Nothing else?' he asked quietly after what seemed to her a rather ominous silence.

'No. What else is there?' she asked with careful neutrality.

'Forgiveness. Getting to know you, you me. Starting again.'

'No,' she said with quiet firmness.

'Why? Why, O'Malley?' he asked quietly, coming to stand behind her, his hands resting loosely on her shoulders. When she didn't answer, he turned her round to face him. 'Why?'

'Because I see no point, because you aren't the man I thought you were.'

'Because I kidnapped my own daughter?'

'No.'

'Why, then?'

'Does it matter?'

'Yes.'

Giving a faint sigh, she looked into his eyes. Right at that moment she wasn't sure what she felt. Mistrust of her own feelings, confusion, want. He could still stir her, make her want him, and if she did as he said and he behaved as he had at the beginning, all those feelings would be rekindled. But he had hurt her, he had said all those things and had believed them to be true. Whether he believed them or not now was immaterial, he had said them and she wasn't totally convinced in her mind that they hadn't held a basis of truth. Despite Nick's reassurances. 'To thine own self be true', but at the moment she wasn't altogether sure who she was. 'Because I've changed,' she said simply. 'I don't know what it is you're asking, a relationship, whatever, but I no longer have the confidence, the ability to believe that I could—satisfy you. When I first met you, you seemed everything that I ever wanted in a man, and whether arrogantly or not, I didn't stop to consider what sort of woman you might want in return. It wasn't exactly a game, more a sort of awareness, a beginning. I didn't consciously analyse where we would go from there, just that I enjoyed your company, wanted you to make love to me,' she said with total honesty.

'And you don't now?' he asked softly, his eyes intent on hers.

'Yes. Part of me, at any rate, but not the whole of me, not like before. If you did nothing else, you at least knocked some of the arrogance out of me.'

'It was your arrogance I liked. And your honesty, your laughter, your courage, your belief in yourself. When I first met you I felt an overwhelming attracttion. You were my sort of person—honest, straightforward, full of humour and courage. For the whole of my life it had been one disaster after another. Things I thought black turned out to be white or a dirty shade of grey. I seem to have lurched from one hell-hole to another, and after my experience with Anita I was afraid to trust my judgement. You were a complication I didn't need. And then Stavros came back with tales of the newspaper woman, and it all fell apart again. Part of my anger was at myself for being so gullible, so stupid as to believe it could all be different.'

'And your words only served to convince me that they must be based on truth. That you saw something in me that no one else had had the courage to point out because I was probably too arrogant to listen,' she murmured. 'I truly didn't expect to see you again, had decided to forget you.'

'And did you?'

'No,' she whispered, her voice a husky thread of sound. 'But I'm working on it,' she added bravely, with a touch of the old O'Malley.

'Is that final?'

'I don't know,' she whispered bleakly.

Staring up into his eyes, she shivered as he ran a gentle thumb across her chin, then in a voice devoid of emotion, he said softly, 'Everything I touch, I destroy. Pray for Jenny, O'Malley. Pray I don't destroy her, too.' Turning quickly on his heel, he went out, closing the door softly behind him. She heard the murmur of voices as he presumably took his farewells of Nick, heard Jenny's childish chatter in the hall, then the front door closing. It had a very final sound. She wasn't aware that she was crying until Nick took her in his arms and wiped her tears away.

'I love him,' she said brokenly.

'And you couldn't tell him?'

'No,' she whispered. 'I didn't know what he wanted in return.' And that was the truth, she realised, she had been afraid of it being thrown back in her face.

She stayed with her father for the simple reason that she couldn't face being alone in her flat. Luc's final words haunted her. He had sounded so lost. Empty, as though meeting her again, talking to her, had been a turning point, a beginning, as though he had needed her. But for what? She had learned a lot about him since his visit, from articles she had hunted out, from Nick, even a book that Luc had written five years before—but they told her very little. Nick introduced her to a friend who had worked with Luc before his marriage, and she learned that his parents had died when he was young. That he had been brought up by an elderly aunt. A close friend had died in his arms in Beirut when a shell had exploded near where they were filming. His wife had died without his knowlege, his daughter kidnapped. 'Everything I touch I destroy.' It made her life look like a fairy-story.

Before she even learned of the exhibition of his photographs to be held in a gallery in the Brompton Road, she had decided she would go to him. For whatever reasons he had sought her out, she needed to see him again, make it right, and whatever the outcome, even if it wasn't what she wanted or needed, then she would accept it and go on from there. He lived in France, she knew, somewhere in Normandy. Nick had his address—presumably Luc had given it to him. For a reason? So that she could find him? She scolded herself for anticipating. One step at at time, O'Malley, she cautioned herself. One step at a time. Just because Nick had once told her she gave off a warmth that people wanted to be close to, it didn't mean that Luc wanted that warmth. He had his daughter now. Yet hadn't he asked for forgiveness? A starting again?

All the changes that had taken place within her over the weeks since she had first met Luc—the introspection, her examination of herself to discover why she did things—gradually disappeared as she began to realise that she preferred the old O'Malley. Certainly her father did; even Ellen, who usually kept her opinions firmly to herself, had remarked that she was glad O'Malley was feeling better. Exchanging a rueful glance with her father, she suddenly laughed.

'Be yourself, darling,' he told her, 'So, you make mistakes, everyone does, but it's no good trying to go against your nature. You were put on this earth as you are, not as someone else. And all you're doing is making everyone else miserable as well as yourself. You were meant to smile, O'Malley. Meant to have the gift of laughter. There's enough gloom and doom in the world without you adding to it! Be yourself!'

CHAPTER EIGHT

IT WAS nearly two weeks since Luc's visit, and the June weather hadn't improved any, there was still a fine drizzle to bead her hair, dampen the classically tailored grey pin-striped suit. O'Malley's face was carefully made-up, bronze shadow deepening her brown eyes, beige highlighter accentuating her cheekbones, a soft rose lipstick warming her generous mouth. She looked stunning, and a great many heads turned to watch her as she strode along the wet pavements. She'd just come from an interview with the chairman of one of the major whisky companies who needed a personal assistant, and she had been offered the post there and then. She had asked for a few days to think it over, which had surprised him, and her mouth twisted in a wry smile. The poor man hadn't been able to understand why she hadn't jumped at the chance. People didn't normally go for an interview unless they intended to take the job offered. Only, before she gave him a firm answer, she needed to see Luc. Or Paget, as she still thought of him. But first, she wanted to see his photographic exhibition.

Closing her umbrella and shaking the drops from it, she pushed inside the gallery. Propping her umbrella by the door, she stared round her. The walls were

covered with black and white photographs, some
framed, others just tacked to boards. There were only
two other people in the gallery, American tourists
judging by their accents, and she cursed their intrusive
tones under her breath. She wanted to be alone, to
look and absorb Luc's photographs in silence. The
lighting was dim, deliberately so, she guessed, to give
more impact to pictures that for the most part were a
harrowing reminder of war. Children, women, their
faces depicting the grief and pain they had suffered.
Anger, too, in some cases. Vietnam, the Far East,
South Africa. Yet not all were of sorrow, she saw. As
she reached the far end of the gallery, there was a
photograph of a young boy, mounted on an easel. He
was laughing. Liquid brown eyes gleamed with
merriment, the black face split by a wide, white,
infectious grin, and she felt her own mouth curve in
response. He was sitting in the middle of a pile of
rubble, devastation all around him, yet his little arms
were held against his tummy as though laughing so
much made his ribs ache.

'That's why I like you,' a soft voice said from so
close behind her that his breath stirred her thick hair.

Turning slowly, her breath held, she stared wide-
eyed at Luc.

'Hello, O'Malley,' he continued, his voice still soft,
hushed almost, and the accented tones sent the
familiar shiver down her spine. His beautiful eyes were
serious as they stared deeply into hers. His hair had
now been professionally barbered, she noted
absently—and he looked devastating. Tanned and
fit—tense? The skin across his high cheekbones

seemed more taut, the jaw more rigid.

'His family had been killed, his house flattened, yet he could still laugh. Like you. In the ruins. Beautiful, disruptive O'Malley, who in the midst of Armageddon could laugh and tease, make jokes . . .'

'Why was he laughing?' she asked huskily.

'George Brent, the man with me, had just fallen down a hole. He was so busy filming, he didn't look where he was walking and wham! One minute there, the next gone.'

Smiling faintly, her eyes holding his, an entirely different conversation going on between them mentally, she asked softly, 'Was he hurt?'

'No. Only his pride.'

'I'm glad.'

'Yes. Nick said you were looking for work.'

'Yes. You've seen him?'

'Mm. This morning. He told me you were coming here. I left Jenny with him. I have a vacancy, O'Malley.'

'You do?' she breathed.

'Yes, looking after a six-year-old girl. Would that be suitable, do you think? I believe I heard that you were once a nanny.'

'Yes,' she mumbled, her voice barely audible, her eyes still locked magnetically with his.

'Plenty of foreign travel, sport, swimming, bed and board, almost unlimited funds.'

'It sounds—interesting.' Then, taking her courage in both hands, she whispered huskily, 'I'm a little tired of temporary work. I was looking for something more permanent, a challenge.'

'Definitely a challenge—and certainly a long-term arrangement.' Then, his voice thickening, he added, 'There's a possibility there may be more children, and then there's the father to look after—did I mention that?'

'No,' she murmured, her heart beating an uneven tattoo in her chest.

'He can be—difficult, bad-tempered, not to say rude. He also jumps to conclusions and says things, lies really, in anger to hurt; he lashes out blindly.'

'Does he have humour? Compassion? Strength?'

'It has been known, on rare occasions, but with the right tutor, those occasions could become more an integral part of his character. He's beginning to learn humility. Not before time, admittedly. He would also need as much, if not more, loving than his daughter. Constant attention at night—he doesn't sleep too well, you see.'

'He doesn't?' she asked faintly.

'No. Will you consider it, O'Malley?'

Swallowing the lump that had formed in her throat, she nodded; she didn't think her voice would work very well.

'You'd be required to take up your duties straight away,' he continued softly, and she shivered again as he put out a hand to gently touch her cheek.

Turning her face into his palm, her eyes still on his, she whispered, 'Is there a trial period?'

'No,' he breathed, his face closer. 'But I could give you a few examples of what would be required.'

'Yes. I think I would need to know,' she whispered back, a spreading warmth inside her making her weak, boneless, her lids heavy.

Moving his thumb to her lower lip, his eyes following the movement, he applied a gentle pressure until her mouth parted. Bending his head, he touched his mouth softly to hers—and she jerked back in shock as a current of electricity shot down to her toes.

'Oh, Luc!' she husked, giving a soft gurgle of laughter, and he smiled, a slow, deliciously intimate smile that softened his eyes, gave warmth to his face.

'You remembered my name,' he said softly.

'Yes.'

Moving his thumb back and forth across her lower lip until it tingled, his eyes intent on hers, he murmured, 'It only happened once, if you remember.'

'Yes. Does it happen with anyone else?' she had to ask, needing to know, needing to torture herself with the knowledge that he had kissed other women, made them react as she had.

'No. Only you, O'Malley.' And she smiled gratefully. Bending his head again, he trailed a featherlight kiss across her mouth, and she groaned, her breath jerking unevenly. He was shaking, just slightly, tremors were transmitted to her through his palm, and with an incoherent little cry she slid her arms round him and raised her face in urgent plea, eyes closed tight. Both were shaking now and had to clutch each other as his mouth captured hers in longing and need. It was a kiss that went on a long, long time, for ever, as hands feverishly touched, mouths clung, parted, only to cling once more, their bodies tight against each other as they fought to get closer still. With a soft oath, he wrenched his mouth from hers, only to pull her impossibly tight into his hold, his mouth on her hair.

'O'Malley,' he murmured thickly, 'I'm sorry.'

'It doesn't matter,' she comforted. 'Not any more.' And it didn't. She wasn't going to waste any more days and weeks trying to find answers when she didn't even know the questions. He was right for her. She needed him. In all his moods, she needed him. As it had been for her father and mother, so it was for her. One man, one life. Smoothing her palms down his back, she revelled in the strength and feel of him, the scent, the power—until, taking a deep, ragged breath, she pulled back to look up into his face.

'Are you sure?' she whispered.

'Yes,' he said simply. 'I've never been more sure of anything in my life. I knew the first time we looked at each other in the cab of the truck—I should have had the courage of my convictions then, only I allowed my mistrust, my cynicism if you like, to cloud my thinking. I didn't believe anyone could be that perfect. Not for me. My life didn't deal me hands like that. I couldn't believe that I had finally found someone who was everything I'd ever wanted.'

'I need you, Luc. I need you very badly,' she said, her eyes fixed on his as she sought to convince him of her honesty. 'There's never been anyone for me, never anyone who could make me feel as you make me feel just by being there, looking at me. I found it so hard to believe I acted the way I did with a virtual stranger. So wantonly. I . . .'

'Excuse me.' At the impatient, rather whiney tones, both O'Malley and Luc turned blankly round.

'Are any of these for sale?' asked the woman, waving a heavily bejewelled hand to indicate the pictures.'

'No,' Luc murmured flatly before turning back to O'Malley. 'Let's get out of here.'

Capturing her hand, curling his fingers warmly round hers, he tugged her from the gallery. Neither noticed the light rain as they walked hand in hand along the road, and both remained silent, thinking their own thoughts. So many questions were whirling in O'Malley's head, but most of all was the knowledge that he wanted her to bear his children, live with him. Giving a long, happy sigh, she turned to look at him. He was so beautiful. Untangling her fingers from his, she tucked her hand in his arm and hugged it tight to her side. Halting, he stared down into her rain-washed face and smiled. A warm, gentle smile, that made her heart race.

'Not changed your mind?' he asked softly.

'No.' A smile curving her own mouth, she put up a hand to trace his cheek and chin. 'You're all wet,' she murmured stupidly, and her eyes suddenly widened in recollection. 'I've left my umbrella at the gallery!'

Laughing, he hugged her to him for a brief instant, then asked huskily, 'Want to go back for it?'

'No,' she whispered. 'I like walking in the rain, feeling it on my face . . .' Then she tailed off lamely as she registered the intent expression in his darkened eyes. 'What?' she asked.

'I want to be alone with you, O'Malley,' he breathed thickly. 'I want to make love to you. Now.' And her breath lodged somewhere in her throat. A most awful weakness invaded her lower abdomen, and her knees most definitely trembled as she just stared up at him, for once in her life totally lost for words.

'After you'd gone, the image of your face with the crushing hurt that I'd inflicted haunted me, and all I could think was, now I'll never know how it would have felt to have O'Malley in my bed. I'd never have those impossibly long legs wrapped round me, never have that generous mouth glide with exquisite pleasure down my body.' And his voice was so thick, it was barely audible. 'I'd never . . .' Breaking off, his nostrils pinched, his eyes tight shut for a moment, he suddenly turned on his heel, put two fingers in his mouth and let out a piercing whistle—and a taxi glided to a smooth halt beside him.

Staring at him in utter stupefaction, not even sure if she hadn't imagined his passionate words of a few seconds ago, she exclaimed in weak admiration, 'I've always wanted to be able to do that.'

'I'll teach you,' he said huskily as he ushered her inside. 'Among other things.' Then, to the driver, 'Sheraton.'

'Sheraton Park Tower?' she asked with a frown.

'Yes.' His voice was almost terse, and she stared at him worriedly.

'Luc?' she whispered. 'What's wrong?'

'Don't ask,' he muttered.

'But I . . .' And then she had her words smothered as he dragged her into his arms and buried his face in her hair—and he was laughing, she discovered, his large frame was actually shaking with laughter.

'Luc!' she muttered in exasperation. 'If there's a

joke, I do wish you'd share it!'

Removing his face from her neck, he stared down at her, his eyes gleaming with humour and something else which she couldn't quite define, then blinked in astonishment as he picked up her hand and deliberately placed it against his groin. Her eyes wide, a delicate pink washed into her face before she too burst out laughing.

'Oh, Luc.'

'Quite. The middle of Brompton Road is hardly the best place to become aroused. So if you have any feeling for me at all, please, O'Malley, just sit quietly and look out of the window or something.'

With a little gurgle of laughter, she did as he said, her own shoulders shaking spasmodically, and then she sobered and warmth filled her. If he could become so aroused just talking about making love to her, what the hell was it going to be like when he actually touched her?

'Was it . . .? Does it . . .?' she began in confusion.

'No,' he said bluntly with a little snort of disgust for his lack of control. 'Not since I was about sixteen, anyway.'

'Well, it's—um—rather comforting that I can at least turn you on,' she murmured wickedly, relishing thoughts of him as a teenager. 'I do hope it lasts until we get to the hotel.' Which reminded her, if he hadn't worked for some time—which presumably he couldn't have done if he'd been searching for his daughter—where did his income come from? Had Stavros been supporting him? Then she denied the thought; Luc was much too proud to borrow from his friends, even if that friend was a millionaire, but she didn't quite know how to ask if he could afford to stay at the Sheraton. Not that the state of his finances mattered, it didn't, or only in so much as should she offer to go out to work?

'Luc? You could stay at the house,' she began worriedly.

'Something else we have to discuss,' he said gently, as though he understood perfectly what she was trying to say.

'I didn't mean to pry,' she said hastily.

'Ah, don't. Don't remind me of my obsessive behaviour before. Whatever there is of my life you want to know, don't ever be afraid to ask. Please. No secrets, O'Malley. Promise?'

'I promise. I just didn't know—well, if you could afford it. I mean, I don't even know if you came to London expressly to see me. Bit presumptuous of me to assume so, but . . .'

'But you know very little about me,' he said gently touching his knuckles to her cheek. 'And yes, I did come to London expressly to find you.' Then, giving a little grin that crinkled his eyes, he admitted a trifle sheepishly, 'But while I was here, it seemed silly not to transact some business at the same time.'

'Like the exhibition?'

'Mm. My agent has been on at me for ages to hold one, only I never wanted to until now. They were reminders of a past that didn't hold any good memories, only now they don't matter, because hopefully, I have a future.' O'Malley's throat blocked with tears again. She could hardly bear to think how grey his life had been compared to hers.

'When you came before,' she murmured huskily, her beautiful eyes fixed on his, 'those things you said, about everything you touched you destroyed, haunted me. I felt so awful, as though it were my fault, for not understanding, not being what you wanted me to be. I was going to come out to France to find you. Is that what you wanted?'

'Yes. I didn't want to rush you, O'Malley. I didn't know how you would feel after the way I behaved. I didn't know how you would feel about Anita, Jenny; I thought I should give you a little time to think about it, be sure. Only I couldn't wait. I flew back to France and spent the most god-awful couple of weeks of my life convinced that I wouldn't be able to persuade you. So I flew back. Apart from which, I got so fed up with people telling me how stupid I was. Stavros, your father. He tore a hell of a strip off me, did he tell you?'

'No,' she said, smiling at him. 'Sounds like Nick, though. Never could mind his own business.'

'But if I could bring Jenny up half as well as he did you . . .'

'Thank you,' she said softly, giving him a lovely warm smile. 'You should tell Nick that, he'd be tickled pink.'

'Ahem. Were you actually wanting to get out here, sir?' the taxi driver said, finally managing to capture their attention.

Peering through the window, they both laughed. 'How long have we been sitting here?' Luc asked him.

'All of five minutes,' he said drily. 'No skin off my

nose—the clock's been running,' he informed them with a grin.

Taking out his wallet, Luc paid him, then added a generous tip. Ushering O'Malley out, he hurried her into the hotel. As he collected his key, she smiled to herself as one of the bell boys rushed to press the lift button for them—Luc was no doubt a generous tipper—then chuckled as he proved her right. They had the lift to themselves, and she turned to stare at him, hardly able to believe that it was all going to be all right. Leaning back against the side, she ran her eyes over him, from the damp tousled hair, to the beautiful eyes, arrogant nose, sensuous mouth and the hard, straight body. 'I love you,' she said simply. If that wasn't what he wanted to hear, she didn't care. She had a need to say it. A need to prove it.

'Do you?' he asked, his voice cracked, his eyes dark, almost black in the dim lift as he leaned against the opposite side, facing her.

'Yes. I've never said that before, or only to Nick, and that's different, a different sort of love. I want to protect you, keep you safe, make you smile, laugh. I want to be held by you, cuddled when I feel sad—and I want to make love with you—I want you to touch me in all the ways a man can touch a woman,' she finished, her voice thick and husky, a mere thread of sound. Her throat felt dry and her eyes too big for her face—and she felt faint. When he only continued to stare at her, his face drained of colour, she also felt sick. Wasn't that what he wanted from her? 'I had to say it,' she whispered painfully, her eyes suddenly bleak, 'because that's what I feel. I can't pretend,

Luc. I can't.'

Before he could answer, if indeed he had been going to answer, the doors whispered open and O'Malley stumbled blindly out into the thickly carpeted corridor.

He took her arm in a grip that felt too fierce, and she was forced to awkwardly follow his striding figure. He fumbled with his key in the lock, and cursed softly, and then they were inside and he was leaning back against the door, his head thrown back against the dark wood. His grip on her arms didn't lessen.

'You choose the damnedest places to say things, O'Malley,' he said on a deep indrawn breath. With a groan, he dragged her tight against him, one hand pressing against her buttocks, and she felt his arousal for herself.

'Oh, Luc, you scared me half to death,' she murmured, collapsing against him in limp relief. 'I thought . . .'

'What the hell do you think you just did to me?' he exclaimed raggedly. Wrenching her back, he stared down into her face. 'Do you think I even dared hope you would love me? The most I hoped for was friendship, warmth. Oh, O'Malley, I don't know what the hell to say.'

'Just tell me you love me,' she said simply. 'Do you?'

'Yes. Oh, yes,' he growled. 'I've waited thirty-eight years for you, O'Malley—and now I'm terrified of losing you.'

'Think I'm not?' she breathed. 'You're a very powerful, sexy man,' she murmured, running her palm across his hard chest. 'Suppose I'm—inadequate?' And he suddenly relaxed and grinned at her.

'Suppose I am?'

'Yeah,' she teased, her voice thick. 'That would be a shock, wouldn't it? Let me tell you, Luc Deveraux, I'm expecting a great deal from this first encounter. The French have a terrific reputation as lovers. Think of the cultural shock I'll experience if . . .' Only his mouth cut off the rest of her words, and her heart somersaulted lazily. Pushing her arms up to his neck in urgent haste, she slid her fingers beneath his hair to rub sensuously against his scalp, warmth and pleasure filling her.

He unbuttoned her jacket and slid it from her shoulders and, his mouth not leaving hers, he tossed it in the general direction of the chair he knew to be there. He undid her skirt and she stepped out of it. Her silk shirt followed, and she shivered as cool air touched her flesh. Moving her hands to his chest, she attempted to undo the buttons of his shirt, then mumured against his mouth, 'Oh, Luc, I'm shaking so much I can't.'

Moving his mouth to the cord in her neck, then her shoulder, he did it for her, and she gained some comfort from the fact that he was shaking as badly as she. As he straightened and removed his shirt, tossing it to join the growing pile on the chair, he stared down at her, then slowly unclipped her bra and drew her tightly against him so that her nipples just brushed his chest.

'Oh, hell,' she whispered, dragging in a deep, shaky

breath.'

'Yeah.' He didn't seem to be breathing at all. 'O'Malley, I think I'm about to pass out,' he muttered thickly. Then, with a shaky grin, he slid his warm hands down over her ribcage to rest intimately on her hips. 'Nearly there.' Taking her by surprise, he picked her up and carried her to the bed, where he lay her gently on the coverlet. His eyes holding hers, he kicked off his shoes, removed his socks, unzipped his trousers and tossed them negligently behind him, and she found she could no longer keep her eyes on his.

Her breath held painfully tight in her chest, she looked down over his strong muscled chest, his waist, and then groaned as he removed the last of his clothing. 'I think the pride of France is safe,' she managed with a great deal of difficulty, and then he was kneeling beside her, unclipping her stockings and rolling them with slow enjoyment down her long legs.

'Such beautiful legs, O'Malley,' he murmured throatily. 'Such beautiful, beautiful legs.' And his accent seemed more pronounced, sexier, the most beautiful voice she had ever heard. He dealt swiftly with her suspender belt, and then only her panties remained. Sliding his thumbs beneath them so that they rested against the hollows formed by her pelvis, he slowly drew them down, and his mouth trailed with frustrating slowness from her navel to her groin—and then he proved beyond a shadow of a doubt that all that was said about Frenchmen was true, and then some.

Despite her own arousal, he wouldn't be hurried and made love to her with a slow mastery that left her exhausted. There wasn't a part of her that he didn't touch with his mouth and hands, nor an inch of him that she didn't explore with sensuous pleasure until need and desire and painful frustration nearly drove her insane—and only when she thought she could take no more did he slide easily inside her and show her that she could.

They lay for a very long time just holding each other, their breathing only gradually returning to normal, and O'Malley knew that nothing in her life had ever prepared her for what had just happened, knew that very few people ever experienced what she experienced. She felt cocooned in a magic spell, a spell she didn't want to be broken. Whatever happened to them in future, nothing could take that away; then suddenly she became aware that he was watching her, his face still.

'Hello,' she said huskily, then had to clear her throat when the word came out all distorted.

'Hello.' And she was pleased to note that his voice didn't sound any better. 'I don't think I believe that happened,' he murmured.

'Want to do it again?' she whispered.

'Yeah. And again and again and again,' he growled. Moving swiftly, he rolled on top of her, then adjusted his body to fit hers exactly so that they were practically nose to nose. She wriggled her hips to get it just right, then gasped as his body responded.

'O'Malley? Will you promise me something?' he asked seriously, his eyes deep and intent on hers. 'Promise you'll never let anything happen to you.'

'Oh, Luc!' she whispered, her eyes filling with tears.

'I don't think I could live without you. You will marry me, won't you? Come to live with me in France? Or if not in France, anywhere you choose.'

Wherever your home is,' she said simply. 'Wherever you are.' Putting up a hand that trembled, she pushed back the lock of dark, silky hair from his forehead, her hand tender, gentle.

'O'Malley?'

'Yes?'

'Have there been many lovers for you?' And she knew by the strain in his voice that it mattered terribly to him.

'No,' she said gently. 'Despite the impression I'm apt to give,' she murmured teasingly as she remembered his words in Turkey, 'there has only ever been one. When I was twenty. It was awful, quite disastrous. Might have put me off for life if Nick hadn't made me believe that, as it was for him, it would only work if I loved. As it has,' she concluded softly. 'After that I just went out with men who were safe, undemanding.'

As he closed his eyes and took a shaky little breath, she deliberately changed the subject, knowing he needed time to come to terms with her words. 'Tell me about your home. About where we'll live.'

Smiling faintly, kissing the tip of her nose, he rolled away from her and sat up. Pushing a pillow behind his back, he pulled her up and into his arms. Snuggling comfortably against him, one leg resting across his strong thighs, she smoothed her hand across his stomach, fascinated by the contracting muscles. 'I own a golf club,' he began, and she stared at him in astonishment.

'A golf club?'

'Mm. Which also has tennis courts, a pool and an old château. I live there most of the time now. When Anita was alive, I put a manager in because she didn't want to live there. She couldn't speak the language——'

'Neither can I,' she remarked drily.

'No. But unlike Anita, it doesn't bother you, does it?' He grinned, knowing very well that she would cope even if she had to learn Serbo Croat.

'No.' She grinned back. 'Shall I be a Lady of the Manor? I think I could quite get to like that.'

'Madame of the Château, at any rate. I take it you are going to make an honest man of me?'

'You'd better believe it. If you think I'm going to let you escape now—let some other floozie have the run of this magnificent body—you are very mistaken, my lad.' And she allowed her hand to wander lower, until he clamped his own hand very firmly over hers and moved it back to his chest.

'You won't mind taking on Jenny?' he asked, and his voice changed, sounded hesitant. O'Malley looked up at him.

'Oh, good heavens! I haven't got to take her on as well, have I? I thought we could put her in an orphanage—or if the Château has cellars, or dungeons yet . . .'

'All right, all right, I'm sorry. Silly question, only I seem to be taking rather a lot for granted.'

'If there's something I don't like, I'll tell you. My

confidence didn't take that much of a bashing,' she quipped. Which was a lie, because it had, but now that she knew he loved her she could be herself, although judging by the gentle smile in his eyes he knew very well how much of a bashing her confidence had taken. Smiling warmly at him, she dropped a kiss on his chest. 'Go on.'

'I had money left me by my grandmother, which I invested. I earned quite a good income as a photographer, and then there were the proceeds from my book. Anita and I bought a house in St John's Wood, which I've since sold. In fact, I used up most of the proceeds searching for Jenny.' Grinning at her, he murmured softly, 'I have a yacht and a fancy car. But, sadly, no designer jeans.' And O'Malley gurgled with laughter as she remembered her taunts in Turkey.

'What I'm trying to say is that we won't starve.'

'I know that. Even if we didn't have any money, we'd manage.' Giving him a warm hug, her fingers sliding round his back, she suddenly touched the long scar and she stared up at him in query. 'How?' she asked.

'Bullet,' he said laconically, and she blanched. 'I was in the wrong place at the wrong time.'

'You could have been killed,' she whispered, horrified.

'No.' He smiled. 'I hadn't met you yet . . . and loath as I am to move, I think Nick might be beginning to wonder where we are. I told him we'd be straight back when I'd found you.'

'Yes. And Jenny. Poor little sausage has had enough upsets in her life. You mustn't worry her by staying away too long.'

'No. Thank you, O'Malley.'

'For what?' She smiled.

'For understanding. For loving me.'

'Don't!' she said fiercely, startling him. 'Don't ever thank me for that! It's my pleasure—and my need! My gift,' she said more softly, feeling rather foolish, yet she did think of it in that way, as a gift, as his love was to her. 'But you mustn't ever leave me,' she whispered.

'No.'

'Nor any other women. I couldn't take that, Luc.'

'Do you think there is any woman alive who could make me feel the way I feel now?' he asked thickly. 'Love me the way you just did? Oh, no, O'Malley—there will be no other women.'

Closing her eyes tight for a moment, and swallowing the lump in her throat, she managed a shaky grin.

'Want me to shower you?' he teased, changing the subject as she had a few moments earlier. 'You've no idea how much I've longed to. In Turkey I suffered the frustrations of the damned imagining you in that wooden tub—and on the island, every time you changed my bandage I wanted to drag you into the bed.'

'And you with the sheet always draped so modestly,' she teased.

'Yes! And you should know why! Especially after that little incident in the Brompton Road!'

Laughing, she traced her finger gently along the still angry scar on his thigh, and her expression sobered.

'I think that frightened me more than anything,' she murmured. 'I hadn't the faintest idea what to do. And I never did take that first aid course,' she added, smiling faintly.

'There'll be time,' he said softly. Tilting up her chin, he pressed a warm kiss on her mouth. 'Time for lots of things—only not now,' he said ruefully.

'No, not now.' Giving a happy, contented sigh, she scrambled to her feet and held her hand out to him. 'Come along, then—bathy time.'

Grinning, he moved more slowly, then scooped her up in his arms and carried her into the bathroom.

Heaven only knew what the people in the next room must have thought. They made a hell of a lot of noise.

BETRAYALS, DECISIONS AND CHOICES. . .

BUY OUT by David Wind   £2.95

The money-making trend of redeveloping Manhattan tenement blocks sets the scene for this explosive novel. In the face of shady deals and corrupt landlords, tenants of the Crestfield begin a fight for their rights – and end up in a fight for their lives.

BEGINNINGS by Judith Duncan   £2.50

Judith Duncan, bestselling author of "Into the Light", blends sensitivity and insight in this novel of a woman determined to make a new beginning for herself and her children. But an unforeseen problem arises with the arrival of Grady O'Neil.

ROOM FOR ONE MORE by Virginia Nielsen   £2.75

At 38, Charlotte Emlyn was about to marry Brock Morley – 5 years her junior. Then her teenage son announced that his girlfriend was pregnant. Could Brock face being husband, stepfather *and* grandfather at 33? Suddenly 5 years seemed like a lifetime – but could the dilemma be overcome?.

These three new titles will be out in bookshops from MAY 1989

W●RLDWIDE

Available from Boots, Martins, John Menzies, W.H. Smith, Woolworths and other paperback stockists.

AROUND THE WORLD WORDSEARCH
COMPETITION!

How would you like a years supply of Mills & Boon Romances ABSOLUTELY FREE? Well, you can win them! All you have to do is complete the word puzzle below and send it in to us by October 31st. 1989. The first 5 correct entries picked out of the bag after that date will win **a years supply of Mills & Boon Romances** (*ten books every month - **worth around £150***) What could be easier?

R	D	N	A	L	R	E	Z	T	I	W	S
E	O	N	M	C	H	I	N	A	A	C	C
G	M	U	I	G	L	E	B	N	N	U	O
Y	E	C	E	G	W	H	I	Z	C	B	T
P	D	R	H	S	E	R	I	A	Z	A	L
T	N	S	M	P	E	R	U	N	D	D	A
N	A	W	I	A	T	P	I	I	E	N	N
Y	L	A	T	I	N	A	N	A	N	A	D
N	G	S	T	N	H	Y	D	E	M	L	Q
W	N	O	J	A	M	A	I	C	A	L	A
R	E	L	A	D	A	N	A	C	R	O	R
T	H	A	I	L	A	N	D	D	K	H	I

ITALY	THAILAND	SCOTLAND	SWITZERLAND
GERMANY	IRAQ	JAMAICA	
HOLLAND	ZAIRE	TANZANIA	**PLEASE TURN**
BELGIUM	TAIWAN	PERU	**OVER FOR**
EGYPT	CANADA	SPAIN	**DETAILS**
CHINA	INDIA	DENMARK	**ON HOW**
NIGERIA	ENGLAND	CUBA	**TO ENTER**

HOW TO ENTER

All the words listed overleaf, below the word puzzle, are hidden in the grid. You can find them by reading the letters forward, backwards, up or down, or diagonally. When you find a word, circle it or put a line through it, the remaining letters (which you can read from left to right, from the top of the puzzle through to the bottom) will spell a secret message.

After you have filled in all the words, don't forget to fill in your name and address in the space provided and pop this page in an envelope (you don't need a stamp) and post it today. Hurry - competition ends October 31st. 1989.

Mills & Boon Competition,
FREEPOST,
P.O. Box 236,
Croydon,
Surrey. CR9 9EL
Only one entry per household

Secret Message _____

_____

Name _____

Address _____

_____

_____

_____ Postcode _____

You may be mailed as a result of entering this competition

COMP 6